Demon Wings
The Fires of a Nightmare

By
Chelsea Lynn Charters

Dedication:

For Kaitlyn, Traci, Brenda, Ciera, Kristin, and my mother, Kelly.
Thank you for being hardcore fans of this novel.

I would be lost without your love and support.

Also, a big thanks to my dad, Jeff, for creating the cover.

Table of Contents

Prologue

I was surrounded by darkness, a
dense, unending darkness that tightened
around my throat and mind. I couldn't move
or speak — all I could do was blink as I
searched anxiously for a light in the
enclosing darkness. I wasn't sure where the
darkness had come from or how it had been
birthed, all I did know was that it was and it
remained. Then, the sensation of my limbs
returned and I was able to walk again.

Peering around uneasily, after a few
minutes of stumbling about, I panted
heavily and fell to the ground, exhausted,
the black aura too much for me to bear, as
if the darkness itself was feeding off of my
desperation.

As soon as I'd given up hope, a vivid

orange flame rose out of the blackness, thriving high above my head. I screamed, my eyes burning from the intensity of the fire, and I had to look away, tucking my head between my knees as I took a few deep breaths to keep myself from fainting. As I struggled to remain calm, I pondered the origin of the inferno. It was all so bizarre.

"*Lily ... Lilianna ...* "a voice called out to me from within the flames.

I froze, frightened by the intensity of the voice. There was someone inside the fire? How was that possible? After swallowing my fear, I glanced up cautiously from my hiding spot and focused on the tall flame that burned fiercely in front of me, my eyes gradually adjusting to its intensity. I wanted to call out — to respond ... but my lips refused to budge.

"*Lily, come to me ...* "the voice said.

I gasped when I saw it ... when I saw

2

the face made of fire. A handsome, yet terrifying face stared back at me from the orange inferno, large black eyes watching me closely, as if it were reading my thoughts. I wondered if they could see how terrified I was.

Those same black eyes sparked before the face spoke again. *"Lilianna, do not fear me. Join me inside the flames. Let their warmth caress your soul."*

A sudden surge of courage rushed through my body, and I managed to ask, "Who are you? What do you want with me?"

The man — if he could be called a man — didn't respond. He only smiled at me. My jaw dropped as I watched him emerge from the flames. He was tall, and made completely of fire. Suddenly, as if sensing my discomfort, he shifted into something more realistic — more human — and I gasped at the sight of the gorgeous man standing before me.

3

He was about my age and near six feet tall, with black shoulder-length hair and hypnotizing grey eyes. I blushed from awkwardness when I noticed he was naked. I'd seen a naked man before, but never had I seen one so perfect. I was already shy from his bareness, but then our eyes locked and he grinned at me, his perfect mouth gleaming. I almost fainted on the spot from the beauty of his smile. *But he isn't real,* I reminded myself sternly. He was a figment of the flames — a monster. I knew I couldn't trust him.

The man took a step nearer me and held out his hand. I stared at it longingly, wondering what to do. My once strong willpower had melted into fervent infatuation, and I couldn't help but think of my attraction towards him. As I watched his fingers motion for me to take his hand, I sighed, and before I knew what I was doing, my right hand reached out and grasped his. In an instant, he pulled me into a tight embrace.

I gasped as he yanked my head back to lick at my neck, where he lined my skin with tough kisses. My face burned with embarrassment when I realized he was protruding against my leg. Uncomfortable with my lack of control, I struggled in his grasp, fearing the passion that flared within my own soul.

"Oh, Lily, how long I have waited for you." His thick voice tickled my ear and he kissed my neck again.

I pulled my head back to gaze at the strange man, my cheeks flushed. As much as I tried, I couldn't deny the attraction I felt towards him, and after studying his face, I whispered, "What are you?"

The monster smiled at me and replied, "You know what I am, Lily."

"I don't—" I began to reply, but then I remembered — I remembered this creature embracing me. I wasn't sure how I knew his identity, but I decided it really didn't matter. Terror filled my heart as I stared wide-eyed at the demon, and I found I was on the verge of screaming.

He groaned suddenly and whispered, "You're still so young and frail, Lily — and your purity bewilders me, as it always does."

I frowned, detesting the way his fingers stroked at my skin. I felt nauseous at the thought of such a wicked creature touching me sensually. Writhing against his body, I tried my hardest to free myself of his grasp. "Let me go!" I cried out, fighting him. "Please!"

The demon laughed wickedly at my endeavors and his grip tightened. "Stop it, Lily. Don't be a fool," he told me fiercely. After bringing a warm hand up to touch my cheek, he said, "Now ... how about a kiss?"

I glanced up warily at the sound of his request, meeting his sparkling grey eyes.

His luscious lips curled upward into a smile and it was then that his spell over me broke; it was as if someone had pulled the blindfold off my eyes. I stared fearfully into the now black eyes of the monster that held me. He was no longer a depiction of beauty — his handsome charm had fallen away — and I shuddered, feeling foolish for falling for his guile. What held me now was an appalling creature with a long snout and gigantic black horns that spiraled at the end.

"No!" I screamed with terror, elbowing him in the gut, and I gasped as I was tossed carelessly to the ground. I cried out as pain shot up the entire left side of my body and I cringed when a few tears slipped out of my eyes. I fought to breathe, the pain engulfing me entirely. After taking a few much-needed deep breaths, I tried to sit up, wanting to run, but once again I couldn't move.

As I lay motionless on the ground, his legs came into my view, and I flinched when he bent down to gaze into my eyes. He had changed back into the handsome man he had pretended to be, and for a second I felt my heart pounding with desire for him. However, I ignored the sensation; I would not fall for his deception again. The demon kept silent, and I trembled under the intense look in his eyes. I bit my lip and stiffened when he reached out to stroke my long brown hair.

"Lilianna ..." he cooed. "Why do you cower before me? Do not fear what you can't understand, child."

I don't know why, but I started to cry. Perhaps it was the fear of never escaping this horrible creature, or maybe it was the fierce pain that stung my left side. I figured it was a little bit of both. Tears streamed down my cheeks as my heart hammered painfully in my chest.

Gazing squarely at my face, the demon dropped his hold on my hair and sighed. He rose before me while saying, "Perhaps I should've waited a little bit longer. You are not ready yet."

"Ready for what?" I asked him fearfully.

He smiled a perfect, charming smile before replying, "For as long as I've known you, Lilianna, you always ask the same pointless questions."

I shook my head, confused. "I don't understand what you mean! I don't know you! I never have!"

This demon — or whatever he was — wasn't making much sense. Why did he keep saying that he knew me? I think I would remember meeting a terrifying demon — or his handsome counterpart. Something about this whole thing wasn't right, but it somehow felt oddly familiar. How could that be? As I stared into the dark eyes of the beast, I felt danger settle deep in my gut.

He snickered at my response. "Lily, do

not worry. I will come back for you when you are ready."

I frowned. "Ready for what?" I asked. "What do you want with me?"

He smiled again, seemingly enjoying my torment. "I thought you knew," he replied softly and his eyes flashed when he watched me shake my head. The beast grinned and added, "I want you to bear my child, Lily."

I gasped, my stomach churning at the thought. I'd had many offers before, but this was just surreal. No way in hell would I lay with that ... thing! Narrowing my eyes at him, I spat, "I will never have your child!"

The demon laughed at my disgusted expression and replied, "Funny ... that's what you always say." He reached a hand out to touch my face, but I turned away from him sharply, hiding against my shoulder.

He clicked his tongue against his cheek

petulantly, his eyes changing back to black. "Until next time then, my lovely."

Suddenly, fire engulfed him wholly. He vanished within it and I stared in horror as the flames began to spread, heading straight for me. I tried my hardest to get up off the ground but I was still immobile, and knew I was doomed. As the fire began to lick at my arm, I screamed and my eyes grew wide with fright as the flames swept over my body, burning me.

I screamed in agony until the pain was too great and I passed out, darkness swallowing me again.

"Lily, wake up!"

I opened my eyes slowly, yawning as my senses awakened. It was pitch black in my bedroom and I could barely see, but after rubbing at my eyes, I found my mother sitting on the edge of my bed. I jumped upright and my pulse quickened.

"Mom? What are you ... doing?" I

asked her fearfully, wondering why she waking me in the middle of the night. She looked worn-out wrapped up in her pale blue robe, hair a mess. There had to be a reason why she'd woken me up. Had something happened?

She didn't answer my question and stretched out her hand to feel along my forehead. "You're burning up, Lily," she told me with a frown. "Are you feeling alright?"

I nodded. "Yes, why?"

Her frown deepened. "Lily, you were screaming at the top of your lungs just a minute ago. Your father almost had a heart attack. He thought something horrible happened to you."

"Was I? I'm sorry...." I bit my lip, surprised.

"Yes, you were — and when I came in here, you were flailing about on your bed like you were fighting somebody off. For a second I thought the worst ... but after switching the light on, I realized you were alone in here." My mother sighed then and examined me worriedly. "I didn't want to disturb you, Lily, but when I left your bedroom and stepped out into the hall, you started screaming again. Are you sure you're alright, honey?"

"Yes, Mom. I'm fine." Shrugging, I added, "I must've had a nightmare ... or something."

"You don't remember?" She asked.

I frowned and tried to recall what I'd been dreaming only seconds before, but my mind kept drawing a blank. All I could remember was darkness, miles and miles of darkness.

"No," I told her softly. "I can't remember."

My mother smiled slightly and stood, giving me a soft pat on the shoulder. "Alright then, Lily. If you're sure you're okay—"

"I am," I told her, strongly. "You don't have to worry."

"Goodnight then, dear," she said, kissing the top of my head.

"Night."

Glancing at the alarm clock on my nightstand, I noticed that it was 3 a.m. Boy, was I going to be a happy camper at work tomorrow. I settled back into the many pillows against my headboard and waited for my mother to leave me to my slumber. As she was on her way out of my room, she stopped halfway through the threshold and turned back around to face me.

"Actually, there was one more thing I forgot to mention," she said slowly.

"What was that, Mom?" I replied with a yawn.

Her relaxed expression vanished as she said, "You kept repeating a name. It was odd sounding...." My mother's face went completely blank as she tried to remember the name, and for some peculiar reason, I started to tremble.

"It was — my, what was that name?" She sighed and shook her head. "I can't believe I've already forgotten it. Hold on, let me think...."

As I was about to dissuade her from telling me, my memory was jumpstarted and the nightmare came flooding into my head. I remembered the black surroundings, the fire, and ... the demon. My heart froze. It was his name, the one my mother heard me saying. But he hadn't told me his name ... or had he? I stared fearfully at my mom's lips, dreading to learn the monster's identity.

"Darcamias," she said suddenly, eyes brightening at the success of remembering. "That's what it was. Darcamias ... hmm, it's a very unusual name, isn't it?" My mother shrugged then, as if it were nothing, before she smiled back at me. "Well, goodnight,

Lily."

I opened my mouth to speak, to prevent her from leaving, but no words came out. My eyes grew wide with fear as I watched my mother blow me a kiss from the doorway and leave me alone in the dark. I glanced around, my pulse rapid, feeling foolish for acting so afraid. *It was just a stupid nightmare! It didn't mean anything.* I rolled my eyes and turned over, praying not to fall back into the same dream from earlier. Even if it was just a figment of my imagination, I didn't want to return there again. As drowsiness began to take me, the demon's name echoed in my head up until my eyelids slipped shut and I returned to the darkness' embrace.

Chapter One

It was perfect weather for a swim. Too bad I had to work. I trudged into Unique Java sullenly, wishing I had called out sick. I didn't make a habit of calling out of work, but today I had the king of all headaches and felt a little nauseous. I blamed my mother for waking me in the middle of the night. If only I had gotten more sleep, maybe then I wouldn't be feeling like a cloud of misery were hanging above my head.

Only twelve o'clock in the afternoon and already the coffee house was bustling with undergraduates and hipsters. I stared straight ahead when I passed a table full of Marilyn Manson wannabes, disregarding their catcalls and obscene gestures as I headed straight for the Employees Only door, which led to the break-room. And I always gave the weird ones the benefit of the doubt...

I found Marion and Jax making out in the main hallway. I rolled my eyes at their indiscretion and moved around them swiftly, walking towards the row of lockers in the neighboring room. Those two were on and off again like crazy, and Marion had sworn that she was done with him for good this time. Oh well. It wasn't my place to lecture her about Jax Haughton. Besides, Jax would do something to mess things up between the two of them eventually. He always did.

As soon as Marion caught sight of me, she broke away from Jax and darted in my direction. Her green eyes were dancing as she greeted me with a hug. "Lily!" she yelled happily, squeezing me tight.

"Hi, Marion," I replied with a smile, hugging her in return.

"How was your weekend?" she asked. "Did you do anything fun?"

"No. It was an absolutely boring weekend," I told her with a frown. "I stayed home all day Saturday, and on Sunday Marcus stood me up."

Marion sighed and shook her red head. "Again? What is wrong with that boy?"

I shrugged. "Who knows and who cares? I hope I never see him again."

"But, Lily!" Marion gasped, eyeing me closely. "I thought you really liked Marcus?"

"I did," I told her, placing my purse on the top shelf of my locker. "But Marcus is a world class jackass, and I'm not going to waste my time pining over him when he's banging everyone in Jackson County." I exhaled loudly and reached for the lip balm in the side pocket of my purse. My gaze flickered over at the mirror hanging on the inside of my locker, and as I stared into the brown eyes of my angst-stricken reflection, I

19

delicately applied some cherry lip balm to my pale lips.

"Yeah, he is kind of a player ..." Marion remarked softly.

"Kind of?" I repeated. "He slept with Debbie Lawson on my birthday! I have no idea why I took that creep back in the first place. Just thinking about all of his lies makes my throat burn with anger," I muttered irritably. "Marcus causes me nothing but grief! I don't know why I put up with him."

"You love him, Lily. That's why," Marion replied.

I bit my lip and frowned, wondering if what Marion said was true. How could I love a two-timing dirt bag like Marcus Brantley? Oh yeah, Marcus was outrageously gorgeous. Since the first day I met him it'd been a struggle to resist his charms.

"Well, it doesn't matter how I feel about him anymore," I told Marion firmly.

"I'm putting my foot down now. Marcus and I are over! We're through!"

Marion smiled and gave me a wink. "Sure ya are, Lily. That's what you always say."

I froze, her last sentence striking a chord with me. I didn't know why, but there was something oddly familiar about that phrase. As I fought to remember, the image of a bright flame sprang from an unknown corner of my mind. For a split second, all I could see was orange and yellow burning against a sinister atmosphere. I gasped after the image passed, and gazed at the ground fearfully, fighting to keep myself from screaming. It felt as if someone had pierced a hole through my soul.

"Lily, are you okay?" Marion asked, placing a gentle hand on my shoulder. "You look scared to death."

I glanced at her warily as I fought to calm down. What the hell was wrong with me? I bit my lip and shook my head, wondering why that nightmare kept upsetting me. It's not like it had really happened or anything.

"Lily?" Marion repeated. "What's wrong?"

"I don't know," I whispered. Then, the agony passed and I could breathe again. I shook my head and smiled, relieved that the dreadful sensation was over. Perhaps it had just been an anxiety attack or something.

Gazing squarely into Marion's eyes, I replied, "I'm fine. Just wigged out there for a sec."

"Uh, okay?" Marion said, watching me closely. "Are you sure, Lily?"

"Yeah. I'm good."

I shut my locker door hastily and moved out of Marion's vigilant gaze. If I knew Marion, and I knew her like the back of my hand, she would keep harassing me until I told her about the silly nightmare —

and I couldn't do that. How childish was it to be afraid of a dream? I was twenty years old for Christ's sake.

Without another word, I hurried out into the hall, but not before grabbing one of Unique Java's purple aprons from the coat rack on the wall. After securely tying the loose straps into a knot behind my back, I pushed open the door and walked out onto the main floor. Tugging off the thin black hair band around my wrist, I pulled my dark brown hair up in a bun. I grinned as I passed by Hailey, Unique Java's newest employee. She'd graduated high school last month and this was her first full-time job. Unfortunately for Hailey, all of the "usual" at Unique Java saw her as fresh meat.

I made my way towards the long counter on the far side of the room, where I usually concocted all of the fabulous drinks Unique Java offered. However, as I was about to unlatch the small door and walk inside, Jax placed his hand on my shoulder, causing me to freeze in my tracks.

"Not today, Ms. Mason," he said.

"Huh?" I replied, twisting around to face him. "What do you mean?"

Jax grinned at me and shuffled one of his large hands through his fiery red hair. "Mr. Brewster wants me to make the drinks today, Lil. He said you can take the orders."

I frowned and crossed my arms. "But I always make the drinks, Jax. *Always.*" I eyed him seriously. Everyone knew how much I hated being on the register. Especially the owner, Mr. Brewster.

Jax shrugged and grinned even wider. "I know, sweet-cheeks, but what the boss man says goes."

"Don't call me that," I told him irritably.

He held up his hands and replied, "Sure thing, Lil. Just don't go upsetting Mr. Brewster with this. He's not in the happiest of moods today."

I didn't argue with him, only rolled my eyes and shoved past him. Leave it to Jax to be a complete asshole. Honestly, since the day I met him he always found ways to get under my skin. I didn't know what he had against me, but I'm pretty sure it had to do with me turning him down two years ago. He was so childish, and out of all the employees at Unique Java — and there were quite a few of them — I hated Jax the most.

I took three much-needed deep breaths to steady my nerves before I wandered over towards the cash register, eyeing it with absolute distaste. I wondered what had happened, why Mr. Brewster was torturing me like this. After what had happened the last time, I thought for sure he wouldn't resort to using me for the task again.

It wasn't the ordering that annoyed me, or even handling the money. What I hated the most were the people. I couldn't stand them. They were loud, and rude, and never tipped me enough — or ever. They never knew what they wanted when they walked up to the counter, or knew what anything tasted like. It was the worst place to be in the coffee hut. The only person who liked ringing customers up was Marion, and only because she loved to talk all day long.

As soon as I took my place behind the register, Marion came running out from behind the office door, bopping her head enthusiastically as a fast tune drifted out from the speakers. I grinned as I watched her blow a kiss at an old man reading in one of the maroon armchairs by the bookcases. He simply shook his head at her and glanced back at the book in his lap.

"I love this song!" she cooed, waving her hands cheerfully as she walked over towards Jax, who was standing behind *my* counter mixing a blended drink. It appeared

26

to be the coffee/cookie concoction, one of Unique Java's favorites — mine as well. Oh, how I would kill for one of those.

I smiled at Marion when she passed me by, ignoring Jax as he stared me down from across the room. Really? Could he be any more obvious? He was dating one of my best friends, yet he couldn't keep his eyes off of me. I'd always wanted to tell Marion what a jerk he was, but I sadly realized it wasn't my place. She probably wouldn't even believe me if I told her what had happened between Jax and me before she started working there. Marion always gave everybody the benefit of the doubt — especially Jax.

There weren't any customers for me to assist at the moment, so I began clearing up a few random receipts lying near the register. When that task was finished I was still bored, and I then began cleaning out the drawers underneath the counter, surprised by the vast amount of junk inside them. I was completely preoccupied, and I didn't notice that someone had walked up to the counter and was waiting on me to order. It was only when they placed a hand gently on the counter that I finally acknowledged their presence. I glanced up at the customer, finding myself staring into a breathtaking pair of light grey eyes, and I almost gasped from their intensity.

Removing my eyes from the stranger's, I studied the rest of his face, so handsome it was almost scary. Shoulder length black hair framed his face, and he had a strong, yet pointed jaw. His features were masculine, but still a tad boyish; his complexion was a rich olive shade. I grinned stupidly, finding myself breaking down in his presence. When I realized I was smiling for about a good minute, my cheeks flared with embarrassment.

"May I help you?" I mumbled, finally

looking away.

"Lily, you're in grave danger," the man told me, his features set in stone.

I didn't find it not the least bit funny, and wondered how he knew my name. As soon as I remembered I was wearing it, my gaze drifted down to my name badge and I rolled my eyes at my foolishness. So, he was trying to be cute, huh? Not the best come on I'd ever heard, but I'd overlook it considering his very manly appeal.

"Very funny, guy," I replied, batting my lashes at him flirtatiously. "I think that was the most pathetic pick-up line I've ever heard." I folded my arms across my chest and asked cutely, "So, what'll it be?"

The man placed his other hand on the counter and leaned towards me. "I'm serious," he said, his grey eyes flashing.

I frowned, wondering if he was a mental case. I knew his massive charm was too good to be true. It was common knowledge that all of the insanely hot men were exactly that. Insane.

"Listen," I began, edging back from the counter. "I don't know what your deal is, but it's not funny, okay? Knock it off."

The man frowned and shook his head. He glanced down at the counter before mumbling, "Maybe it was too soon. She's clearly not ready ..."

"Huh?" I mouthed, watching him fearfully. Who was this guy and what did he want with me?

His head shot up suddenly, and I gasped when I noticed that his eyes appeared to be unnaturally wide. I backed away further from him, an unusual sensation settling in the pit of my stomach; it was the same feeling I felt when remembering that stupid nightmare. I stopped reversing when my butt hit the wall, and I cringed when I realized there was only a counter and two feet of tile keeping us apart.

As I stared nervously into the man's bizarre grey eyes, a light bulb went off in my head. My eyes widened in surprise, and I hastily examined the stranger once more. I realized a similarity was there, hidden within the man's striking features. *How could I have missed that before?* My heart trembled, and I fought to breathe while I stared at the same man from my nightmare.

"You ..." I murmured, tears stinging at my eyes. "It's you!" I yelled, causing everyone's head in Unique Java to turn and stare in my direction. Hushed whispering broke out around me, but I didn't care. All I could concentrate on was the monster standing before me.

The man frowned when he noticed the distress on my face, and with a slight bow of his head, he said, "I'm sorry for disturbing you, Lilianna." With a strained smile, he turned away sharply from the counter and walked out of Unique Java.

I watched him pass by the window of the café, and my heart plunged when he stared at me through the glass. He studied me until the window ended, then I breathed a sigh of relief when he was finally gone.

Marion came rushing over to my side as soon as he left, eyeing me carefully. "Lily? What happened? Who was that guy?"

I shook my head and stared at the counter. That was an excellent question, and I found myself wanting to know the same thing. Who the hell was he? Could it be that he was actually the demon from my nightmare? He looked just like him ... he had the exact same eyes. No, it couldn't possibly be true. *It was just a stupid dream! Demons aren't real ... right?*

"Lily?" She said my name with a worried frown. "Who was he?"

I snapped out of my thoughts and glanced back at her, my eyes holding a hint of fear.

"I don't know who he was, Marion," I told her softly. "I don't know."

Chapter Two

"So, you're coming to open mike tonight, right? Jax and I signed up!" Marion told me excitedly. "We're singing *You're So Vain* by Carly Simon." She twirled a finger through her red curls. After studying me for a moment, Marion asked, "You do know that song, right? Please tell me you do. Jax had no idea until I played it for him."

"Yeah, I know it," I replied softly as I swept up chunks of broken cookies and muffin crumbs off of the floor. After pushing the pile of filth into the dustpan with the tip of the broom, I smiled with relief. I glanced around the dimly lit shop, enjoying the peaceful quiet — while trying to ignore the blaring of Jax's earphones.

It was nine o'clock and Unique Java was, thankfully, closed for the night. The only employees left in the place besides me were Marion, Jax, Hailey, and Mr. Bill. Mr. Bill was Mr. Brewster's eldest son, William. He was twenty-nine years old, had a bright yellow ponytail, and was the complete opposite of his father. He liked to be called Mr. Bill because, well, it was simply a cool nickname — and he always said William sounded too formal. Will was hip, wise, and full of energy. He ran the place most of the time, and honestly, Unique Java would not have been as cool as it was if it hadn't been for William's crazy-yet-amazing ideas.

My eyes flickered over at Marion, who was busy wiping down the cashier counter frantically, uttering obscenities and missing the most obvious marks and stains. After the incident with the strange man, she'd stayed by my side the entire night, offering me less than helpful assumptions for his weird behavior. Although she'd most likely made my fear of him worse, I was glad she wanted to comfort me. Marion was silly, but she was a good friend.

"You missed a spot," I told her with a smile as I watched her rub down the register half-heartedly.

Marion's red head shot up, eyeing me distastefully. "I don't care. If we don't hurry we're going to be late. Jax and I have been practicing all week for this! I don't want to miss it!"

I grinned at the mental image of Jax and Marion singing a duet in front of a large crowd. I wondered how horrible they were going to sound. Marion couldn't sing a note, but I wasn't sure about Jax. He might have enough talent for the both of them. I doubted it though.

After bending over to pick up the dustpan, I hurriedly dumped the various food particles into the trashcan, careful that the dirt wouldn't get on my hands. When I straightened up, I caught Jax staring at my rear-end. What a creep. I rolled my eyes, and when Marion's back was turned, I gave him an unpleasant gesture with my hand. With a triumphant smile on my face, I trudged over to the bookshelves to help Hailey reorganize all of the misplaced novels and magazines on the tables.

At that exact moment, Mr. Bill came bumbling out of the back door wearing his black Ray Bans and leather motorcycle jacket. Beneath his jacket, he wore a red mesh shirt, which was completely see-through. I laughed when he gave a high-five to Hailey as he passed us by, who seemed absolutely bewildered to see him in such attire. She would get used to it though. We all had to.

"Time to go, kiddies!" Mr. Bill announced enthusiastically, rushing towards the front door. He removed the keys from his jacket pocket and went to unlock the entrance.

"I have to go get my purse!" Marion replied excitedly, before running towards the employee door. She gave Jax a quick peck on the cheek as she ran past him.

"Mr. Bill, what about the bookshelves?" Hailey asked suddenly, her face growing red when everyone in the shop turned to stare at her.

It was common knowledge to never question Mr. Bill. If he said it was time to leave, then it was time to leave. Obviously she hadn't been listening to me when I explained the "Unique Java Way" on her first day of work. I told her taking notes would've come in handy.

Mr. Bill paused, his hand in mid-air with the key poking out of his thumb and index finger. A few moments passed before he twisted his head to look in Hailey's direction, a noticeably forced smile on his face.

"What was that, Hailey?" he inquired,

his smile faltering. "Something about bookshelves?"

I nudged her shoulder, causing her to cast a glance my way. I said nothing, and shook my head — seriously stern. Thankfully, Hailey got the hint quick.

Hailey swallowed roughly and glanced back at the boss. "Nothing, sir," she replied nervously. "Never mind."

Mr. Bill's tense expression eased up and he finally smiled a genuine smile. After glancing around the shop, he said, "If you have any personal belongings, go get them now. I'm locking this place up in five."

"What's the rush, Mr. Bill?" Jax asked him curiously. When Mr. Bill slowly turned around to face him, Jax added warily, "If you don't mind me asking ..."

"It's open mike night down at Sam's Bar, Jax. I never miss it."

I rolled my eyes at Mr. Bill's fondness for cheap entertainment and headed towards the break room. Why did everyone love open mike night? I knew why Mr. Bill did. Sam's always had a two-for-one special going that night and he couldn't pass up an opportunity like that. Since I couldn't *legally* drink yet, there was no reason I needed to go. I hated listening to people butchering famous songs — or even songs they'd written themselves. To me, open Mike night in Jackson was just like karaoke ... and I hated karaoke.

Hailey trailed behind me into the employee lounge, her blonde head bowed low, looking more timid than usual. I held the door open for her, letting her enter before me. Marion was standing in the middle of the room, changing. My eyes grew wide with surprise when she pulled off her black t-shirt right in front of us, showing off her red lace bra. My gaze flickered over at Hailey, who was still staring at the floor, her cheeks the reddest I had ever seen them.

"Marion? What are you doing? You know we have a bathroom where you can change!" I scolded her sharply. "What if Mr. Bill walked in here? Or Jax?"

Marion unbuttoned her slim black jeans and hastily peeled them down to her ankles. "Mr. Bill won't. He's ready to go. And Jax ... well, he's seen the best of me already," she replied with a wide smile. She slid a hot pink dress over her head, and then reached for the black belt that was lying on the table next to her.

"You have no shame, Marion," I told her, shaking my head as I walked over to my locker. I removed my purse and slung it over my shoulder quickly. After double-checking that I'd grabbed everything I needed from my locker, I breathed a sigh of relief. I couldn't wait to get out of there.

"So, what are you wearing tonight? That cute little blue dress?" Marion asked me eagerly. "Maybe the red one?"

41

I glanced over at her and replied, "I don't think I'm going tonight, Marion. I'm tired."

Marion's enthusiastic expression fell, and she rushed at me, her green eyes dark. "What? Lily, you have to!"

I exhaled loudly and walked around her, heading for the door. "No, I don't, Marion. I'm not in the mood. After what happened earlier ... I'm just not up for it."

Marion frowned and approached me once more. "I know that guy freaked you out, but—"

"You don't even know the half of it," I said her gloomily.

A shiver went through my entire body as I recalled the stranger's peculiar grey eyes — how they'd pierced right through me. I hadn't figured out if that man really was the monster from my dream, or if I was just a psychopath for even considering that theory. I was vastly leaning towards the latter.

"That's why you need to go out," Marion told me slyly, hooking her slender arm around mine. "It'll take your mind off of that weirdo ... and Marcus."

"I don't think—"

"You need a distraction, Lil," she interrupted. "Trust me! It'll make you feel ten times better."

I glanced down at her and smirked. She always knew what to say to bend me to her will. Marion was a sly fox.

"All right, fine!" I exhaled loudly. "But you have to buy my drinks."

"Of course," she replied with a shrug. "Don't I always?"

"Yeah. Because I'm underage," I said with a grin, and reached for my cell phone inside my purse. "I just have to call my parents and tell them I'll be out for a few more hours. Give me a sec."

Marion nodded and walked out of the

room, leaving Hailey and I alone in the lounge. I dialed my home phone number, waiting patiently as the phone rang and rang. No one picked up at home, so I left a short message for them after the beep. As I slid the phone back into my purse, I turned to leave, but I froze when I overheard Hailey crying.

I frowned and glanced over at her. She was slumped against the row of lockers, her arms wrapped around her body tightly, and her long blonde hair covering most of her face. She looked so vulnerable at that moment, and I wondered what had made her so upset.

"Hailey? Are you alright?"

She shook her head and replied, "Everyone hates me."

"What?" I was surprised by her remark. Hesitant at first to approach her that doubt melted away when I realized she was genuinely upset. She needed a friend right now.

"Nobody hates you, Hailey," I told her softly, walking closer towards her. "Why do you think that?"

"Because! I keep messing up! Tonight Mr. Bill looked so angry," she whined, shaking her head furiously. "He's going to fire me! I know he is!"

"He's not going to fire you, Hailey," I told her calmly, joining her by the lockers. "He just likes things done his way. Mr. Bill doesn't like to be questioned."

"I know ..." she replied with a sniffle. Hailey wiped at her tearstained cheeks before adding, "I just wanted to impress him. I thought if I showed Mr. Bill I wanted to keep cleaning, he would think I was a dedicated worker ... or something like that. I'm so stupid."

I smiled at Hailey's comment and pulled her into a warm hug. "You're not stupid, Hailey. It'll be okay. Trust me. Mr.

Bill is going to be so wasted tonight that he'll forget it even happened."

Hailey glanced up at me keenly, her pretty blue eyes red and puffy from crying. "Do you really think so, Lily?"

"Yes. So chin up." I dropped my hold on Hailey and walked over towards the open doorway. "Hurry and get your stuff so we can get out of this place, okay?"

"Kay," she replied faintly.

"And you're coming with me to Sam's tonight. I refuse to listen to Marion's awful singing alone," I told her with a grin.

Hailey beamed at me from across the room; she seemed pleased enough to be invited. I watched as she hurried towards her locker, whipping out her messenger bag and a change of clothes. Giving her some privacy in case she brashly decided to take her clothes off as well, I walked out of the room and down the employee hall, finding Marion waiting for me by the door.

46

"Ready?" she asked me eagerly, her green eyes dancing.

"Yeah." I bit my lip and added, "I invited Hailey to come with us — I hope you don't mind?"

Marion shrugged and replied, "No biggie. It's whatever." She frowned suddenly and looked me over carefully. After gesturing to my clothes, Marion asked, "You're not going to wear that to the bar, are you, Lily?"

I frowned and glanced down at my black on black attire. "Why? What's wrong with it?"

She wrinkled her nose at me before saying, "It's fine I guess ... but it's just so coffee-house beatnik. The only think you're missing is a black beret atop your head."

I laughed and brushed past Marion, rolling my eyes at her haughty remark as I walked towards the entrance. Mr. Bill held the front door open for me with an impatient look on his face, and I quickly said my goodbyes for the night as I stepped out into the cold night.

On the walk over to my car, I wondered if Marion's earlier suggestion would work. There was no doubt in my mind that I could keep my thoughts off Marcus. The strange man on the other hand ... well, that was going to be a little more difficult. I couldn't even forget that stupid dream. How on Earth was I going to forget about *him?* His bizarre grey eyes were captivating enough, aside from the fact that he looked exactly like the demon in my nightmare.

If that man was truly a demon ... no! I couldn't think like that. I had to be a realist. It was just a stupid nightmare □ dreams don't come true. The more I agonized over it, the more pathetic I felt. I should have just listened to Marion and put the odd events behind me. He was probably just some loser searching for kicks. Everything was going to be okay ... I just had to set my mind in the right direction.

Chapter Three

By the time Hailey and I made it to Sam's, the bar seemed to have almost reached its maximum capacity. There was barely enough room to walk around, let alone dance, like some people were doing. After we pushed our way into the middle of the loud bar, we spotted Marion and Jax standing over at the counter. Marion was bopping her curly red head, jiving to the music, while Jax sat slumped over the counter. I realized Hailey and I must have arrived just as open mike was about to begin, because a few men were setting up the stage and fixing the lights.

When Marion saw Hailey and I approach her, she beamed and waved us over ecstatically. "Lily! Hailey! Over here!" she yelled out, flailing her arms wildly while her green eyes twinkled with delight.

I glanced down at Hailey and smiled. This was her "official" first night out with Jax and Marion, and she seemed a little nervous about it. She should be, after all the wild stories Marion had told her. But, no matter how outrageous Marion and Jax were, Hailey was in for a good time.

"Hey, guys!" Marion grinned as she watched Hailey and I walk up to the bar. "I'm so glad you guys are here! We were just about to take some shots." She laughed and turned to grab a readied shot glass from the counter behind her.

When she held the glass out to me, I studied the clear liquid, wondering if it was vodka or rum. I decided it didn't matter, and reached for the shot glass eagerly, downing it in a mere second. I ignored the burning sensation in my throat and gave Marion a wide smile.

"Thanks," I told her. "I needed that."

At the sound of my voice, Jax turned away from the counter and glanced over at me. My stomach lurched with nausea as I watched his blue eyes drink me in.

"You want another one?" he asked, with an intense smile. "My treat."

I frowned at his offer and shook my head. "No, thanks. One's enough."

"Oh, come on, Lil! Live a little!" Marion urged me. "Let Jax buy you one more shot."

"No, I'm good," I replied hastily.

Honestly, I wouldn't have minded taking another shot □ but not if Jax was paying for it. I refused to give him the satisfaction of buying me a drink.

Suddenly, the music died down, and all of the lights in the bar dimmed. A loud screeched erupted from the microphone onstage as Sam Clement, the owner of the establishment, tapped violently on the mike's mouthpiece. Everyone in the bar cringed and covered their ears, just in case.

"Whoa! Sorry about that everybody!" Sam grinned, removing the microphone from the stand. He brought it up near his mouth to say, "How about we get this party started, huh?"

The crowd cheered as Sam introduced the first singer of the night. I watched him with a smile while he provoked the crowd to clap for the newbie guitarist, David Wartz. When David wandered on to the stage, Sam gave him a friendly pat on the back before walking offstage and towards the bar. After rolling up his sleeves, he joined the two other bartenders and began pouring and mixing drinks.

Sam Clement was like a father figure to many of the people who frequented his bar. In his mid-fifties, Sam was a round, jolly man who ... well, to tell you the truth, he actually looked a lot like Santa Claus — minus the red cloak and hat. Sam was a very funny and giving man; he gave away pitchers of beer and food to Marion and me all of the time. He was pretty wealthy — always donating money to charitable organizations like the Jackson County Orphanage and the homeless shelter. I think Sam was so rich because he had no kids of his own. He'd always said his bar was his baby.

When David finished his odd, electric guitar version of T-pain's *I'm Sprung*, he bowed and left the stage, grinning like an idiot as the drunk — and obviously deaf — crowd cheered him on. I rolled my eyes when he boldly kissed one of the tipsy tramps hovering by the stage. Wasn't he getting a little ahead of himself? He only played one song, and already considered himself a celebrity?

Sam walked back onstage, clapping and smiling. I wanted to use the ladies' room before the next musician played, and so I hurried through the thick mass of people, heading for the restrooms in the back of the bar. Thankfully, there wasn't a line, and I got in and out. Before I walked out of the bathroom, I paused by the mirror to examine my reflection.

I stared into my eyes; the mascara I had applied earlier was still holding up nicely. After smoothing down my layered hair, I then searched every inch of my face, hoping my eyes wouldn't fall upon an imperfection. I wasn't vain ... I just suffered from low self-esteem.

Dating Marcus Brantley will do that to you. One minute he'd make me feel like I was the prettiest girl in the world — the next I was wondering how he could sleep with Debbie Lawson, someone who wasn't even in the same league as me. As I stared back at my miserable expression — because my mood always turned sour when I thought about Marcus — I realized it was hopeless. It didn't matter if I looked good on the outside when my inside was such a mess.

I sighed and took a step back from the mirror, and with a forced smile, I headed for the restroom door. The next singer had already taken the stage, but I couldn't see who it was because I was too short to see over the very large bikers standing directly in my path. As the crowd applauded for the next act, I pushed my way back towards my friends, and a familiar voice spoke through the microphone.

My eyes darted towards the stage, narrowing in surprise as they watched my ex-boyfriend grasping the mike in his hands.

"Lily, I know you're somewhere in this crazy crowd," he said, lifting his free hand to shield his eyes from the bright lights. He tried to spot me amongst the many patrons, but gave up when he realized there were too many faces.

"I just want you to know that I love

you, Lil," Marcus added softly. "This song is for you."

Marcus flashed a sparkling grin to the crowd, then he sang the words to "our song" — the song that had been playing in Marcus' car the night we shared our first kiss together. I got a little teary-eyed as I watched him on the stage, singing for me. He was actually pretty decent too. Hearing that song, Foreigner's *I Want to Know What Love Is*, stroked a soft spot in my heart, and I almost wanted to run to the front of the crowd and let Marcus know that I still cared.

Then I remembered how angry I was at him — and that I'd told Marion I was finished with his deceit. As Marcus sang his heart out to me — and milked the crowd — my blood boiled with rage. How naïve was I? After all the shit he'd put me through, was I really just going to roll over for him whenever he came back spouting love lyrics? Like hell I was!

I watched him make love to the crowd, and rolled my eyes before joining Marion and the rest of the group at the bar. When I got back, Marion seemed a little on edge about me disappearing.

"Lily, where have you been?" Marion asked. "You just took off without telling anybody where you were going!"

"I went to the bathroom," I replied slowly, wondering why she was so hyped up. "Why does it matter?"

Marion glanced at the stage and pointed out Marcus. "Marcus is up onstage, Lily! He's singing this song for you!"

"Yeah, I know, Marion," I replied coolly. "I saw him."

"Doesn't that make you happy?" Marion asked me eagerly, her green eyes sparkling. "Aren't you thrilled Marcus is being more romantic?"

I narrowed my brows at her in suspicion. Why did Marion care so much about Marcus being up on that stage? What did it have to do with her? I pondered and pondered until it suddenly popped into my head: Marion had set the whole thing up with Marcus. She didn't convince me to come here tonight to forget about Marcus. *I'm here because she wants me to get back together with him.*

"Marion ..." I huffed. "What did you do?"

Her face flashed with anxiety at my question, but she didn't respond. Marion turned away from me then, playing it off as she tried to flag one of the bartenders down.

"Marion!" I said her name more fiercely this time. She must've realized I was gravely upset, or that I wasn't going to stop badgering her, because she twisted back around to face me with a frown.

"What's Marcus doing here?" I asked her sternly, after peeking over at the stage.

I realized the song was nearing its end, and I would have to face Marcus in a matter of seconds. If that was the case, I wanted some answers first.

Marion shrugged coolly and replied, "I don't know why he's here, Lily."

"You're such a liar," I said, glaring at her.

She flinched at my insult but still held her ground. "Lily, I don't—"

"Just tell me the truth, Marion!"

Marion bit her lip and glanced away before replying, "Lily, it's not that big of a deal." When I didn't show any signs of unrelenting, Marion frowned and shook her curly red tresses. "All right! I'll tell you ..." With an aggravated groan, Marion finally confessed. "I may have mentioned to Marcus earlier that you were going to be here tonight."

"Why would you do that, Marion?" I inquired loudly, grabbing the attention of a few patrons near us at the bar counter. "Why?"

"Yeah, Marion. Why do you care?" Jax spoke up, eyeing her closely. "Who Lily dates is none of your business."

I knew what he was trying to do, but I didn't want his help. It was weird enough that he was taking my side at all.

Marion glared at him "Just stay out of it, Jax! I did what I thought was right!"

I rose my brows at her comment and asked, "How is tricking me into coming here tonight the right thing?"

"Because, Lily ..." She pointed her finger directly at my heart and said, "You love him."

I rolled my eyes at her childish excuse and replied, "It doesn't matter if I love him, Marion! I told you before that I don't want Marcus in my life anymore!"

Marion glanced over my shoulder and said, "Well, if that's how you feel, here's your chance to tell him. He's headed this way."

My face burned with anger as I sharply turned around, watching as Marcus pushed and shoved his way through the thick crowd. I was too angry to be patient — to wait for him by the counter, and so I met him in the middle of the bar.

Marcus' dark eyes sparkled at the sight of me. He grinned, flashing his usual dreamy smile, and reached out to embrace me. I backed away hastily, shaking my head as I crossed my arms. I must have looked less than thrilled, because Marcus' bright smile was reduced to a frown.

"What's the matter, Lily?" Marcus asked, watching me closely.

"Where were you last night? We had a date."

Marcus stared at me blankly, as if bewildered by my question. "No, we didn't, Lily. I would've remembered if we had a date."

I raised my eyebrows at his remark, knowing full well he was lying to me. With an obnoxious laugh, I replied, "Oh really? Then why didn't you pick up your phone? I called you all night and left messages." I paused to take a breath, to ease my tension before I asked, "Where were you, Marcus?"

His eyes flashed with guilt — but only for a second. He shrugged at me and replied calmly, "I was hanging out with Steven and Tony last night."

"Oh really? Steven and Tony?" I mumbled, shaking with rage.

Marcus nodded. "Yeah. Go ahead and call them if you—"

"If I don't believe you?" I finished for him angrily. "Well guess what, Marcus? I don't fucking believe you!"

He took a step back, startled by my obscenity. "What the hell is your problem?"

I folded my arms across my chest and

spat, "You're my problem! I called Debbie Lawson's house last night. Debbie wasn't home, but her mother and I had a nice little chat."

"What's that got to do with me, Lily?" Marcus replied, irritably.

"She told me that you and Debbie went out to see a movie last night."

Panic crept over Marcus' face, and the sight made me burn with triumph. If I had any doubts about him cheating on me with Debbie, they were gone now.

"Exactly," I replied stonily.

"Lily, please ..."

I held up my hand to silence him. "No. I won't do this with you anymore, Marcus. It's over between us."

Marcus frowned. "Don't say that, Lil."

With a sigh, I turned away, heading for the exit — but Marcus' hand shot out and grabbed my arm, preventing me from leaving. I twisted my head to glare at him, while trying to wriggle my arm out of his hold. His grip wouldn't budge though.

"Get your hand off of me!" I told him loudly.

"No," he said firmly. "Let me explain, please."

"There's nothing to explain! You're a lying, cheating son-of-a-bitch — and I'm done playing the fool!" I shouted. I rolled my eyes as I stared at his wounded expression. Marcus always portrayed the victim so well; he never ever took responsibility for his actions.

"Lily—" he began, trying to pull me towards him.

"Just stop it, Marcus!" I interrupted hastily. "Let me go!"

Marcus' grip on my arm tightened as he said, "Nothing happened between me and Debbie. I swear."

"You are so full of shit," I spat, and I managed to yank my arm out of his grasp.

"Can't we talk about this?" he asked me faintly, taking a step towards me.

I back away quickly and shook my head. "No, Marcus. Stay away from me!" I turned to walk off, but I added, "Don't call me, don't text ... just leave me alone."

"You're making a big mistake, Lily," he said suddenly, his eyes darkening. "Once you realize how foolish you've been acting, it'll be too late. I won't be around when you want to come crawling back to me."

"Fuck you," I told him icily, before turning and walking away.

Before I left Sam's, I stopped by the counter to confront Marion about her meddling in my love life. She bowed her head in shame when I walked up to her and I knew by the look on her face that she felt horrible for what she did — but that wasn't good enough punishment for me. She was supposed to be one of my best friends! How could she hurt me this way?

"I hope you're happy, Marion," I said angrily, eyeing her with disgust. "You've actually managed to make my night even worse."

Marion still refused to look at me as she replied, "I'm really sorry, Lily."

"You should be," I told her heatedly.

"Come on, Lily," Jax spoke up, putting his arm around Marion. "You don't have to be so mean to her."

"Are you kidding me, Jax?" I replied hotly. "I told her *today* that I didn't want to see Marcus anymore — yet she still invited him here tonight! She went behind my back and concocted this whole thing!"

Jax glanced down at Marion's hidden face. "I know ... but she just wanted to see you happy. She had no idea Marcus was cheating with Debbie again."

"Whatever," I mumbled, folding my arms. "It still doesn't excuse what she did."

Marion glanced up at me then, and I

noticed that her usual bright green eyes were puffy and red. My heart stung with guilt as I stared back at her grief-stricken expression.

"I know I shouldn't have called him, Lily," Marion told me softly. "I just wanted you to be happy again … I thought maybe Marcus just needed a push in your direction." Frowning suddenly, she added, "And I swear that I didn't know he was still seeing Debbie."

I frowned at her response. Marion was clearly upset about what happened — and ultimately her heart had been in the right place. Besides, I couldn't be angry with her forever; I loved her too much. My anger melted away as I continued to stare at her cute face, and I realized that the battle between us was finally over.

"Okay," I sighed suddenly, walking up to her; I put my arms around her to give her a hug. After placing my chin atop her head,

I added, "Just don't do anything like that again."

Marion nodded and hugged me back. "I promise, Lil."

I glanced over at Hailey, and smiled when I noticed the uncomfortable expression on her face. Poor girl. Maybe I should retract my earlier statement about her having a good time tonight.

"Hailey, is it all right if you catch a ride home with Marion or Jax?" I asked her. "I need to get out of here."

"You're leaving?" Marion interrupted anxiously.

I nodded and replied, "Yeah. I've had enough excitement for one day. I just want to lie down and go to sleep."

"It's fine, Lily," Hailey spoke up, giving me a small smile. "I don't mind."

"I'll take Hailey home," Marion offered.

"Thanks," I told them both softly.

When I made a move to leave, Hailey

placed a warm hand on my arm and said, "I'm sorry, Lily — about Marcus."

I smiled at Hailey, grateful for her sympathy, and after looking over each of them, I said, "See you guys later."

With one last smile at Marion, I turned away from the group and walked out of Sam's.

Chapter Four

"Shit! Shit! Shit!" I screamed in exasperation, slamming my fists against the steering wheel of my sedan.

Leave it to my piece of shit car to fail me right when I was trying to escape from Marcus. I took a deep breath, realizing stressing out would do me no good. Maybe the car would start if I tried just one more time. After replacing the key into the ignition, I braced myself, and tried to start the car again. My heart sank into despair when the same loud churning sound emitted from the engine.

I exhaled loudly, ripped the keys out of the ignition, and grabbed my purse before stepping out of the car. There weren't any other people in the parking lot, and a slight shiver went down my back when I realized I was all alone out there. Instantly, I recalled the incident with the stranger from earlier, and fear took control of my thoughts. I surveyed my surroundings cautiously before retrieving my cell phone from my purse, and then I dialed home. Thankfully, my parents picked up this time.

"Lily, hello?" It was my father on the line.

"Hey, Dad," I replied quickly.

"Honey, is everything all right? We received your voicemail from earlier. Are you still at Sam's?"

"Yeah ..." I said, biting my lip. "I'm still at Sam's, but I was actually on my way home—"

"You'll be home soon then?"

I sighed at his question. "No. My car won't start."

"Oh ... well, do you want me to come pick you up?"

I was on the verge of accepting my dad's offer when Marcus came rushing out of the bar. He spotted me in an instant and hurried in my direction before I could stop him. This was not good. I couldn't get into an argument with him while I was on the phone with my father. My dad didn't like Marcus, and I knew he would've come rushing to my rescue if he overheard the two of us going at it.

"I'll have to call you back, Dad," I told him briskly.

"What? But, Lily—"

"It's okay, Dad. I'll call you back. Bye."

Before my father could get another word in, I ended the call. I pocketed my phone just as Marcus walked up to me, and I noticed he had an odd look on his face. He seemed upset.

"What do you want?" I asked him angrily. "I already said everything that needed to be said."

Marcus looked me over before replying. "I thought you were leaving?" he asked me softly.

"I was — I mean ... I am."

He looked squarely at me and asked, "Why haven't you then?"

"Because ..." I began, crossing my arms haughtily. I searched for a clever excuse to give him, but my mind was drawing a blank. I couldn't tell Marcus my car wasn't starting; he would most likely offer me a ride if I did. I didn't want give him an opportunity to save me.

"It's none of your business!" I finally said, eyeing him rudely. "Just back off!"

"Jesus, Lily," he spat, shaking his head. "Why are you acting so hostile all of a sudden? First you treat me like shit in front of everyone at Sam's for no reason, and now you won't even answer a question without screaming at me!"

For no reason? Was he fucking serious? He'd slept with that slut on my birthday — and like a fool I took him back, believing he would mature and put our relationship first. Obviously that was never going to happen. All Marcus cared about was himself.

"You are unbelievable, Marcus! You really are!" I shouted at him, my eyes narrowed like daggers. "Even after all the hurt you caused me, you won't accept responsibility for what you've done to our relationship."

Marcus frowned at me and replied, "What are you talking about? I haven't done anything wrong, Lil."

My throat burned with anger at his denial. "You had sex with Debbie!" I shot back. "On my fucking birthday! That's what you did wrong! Do you remember that, Marcus?"

With a grunt, he glanced off, staring down the empty street. "I thought you got over that whole thing."

My jaw dropped; I couldn't help it. Of

course I'd never got over it! How could he act so nonchalant about his affair with Debbie? Like it wasn't a big deal that he lied to me for months about seeing her behind my back. I'd known all along — confronted him enough times about it for him to confess. But he never did, and he wouldn't have; I had to catch him in the act to learn the truth. It was as if he was oblivious to his mistakes, and whatever pain he put me through wasn't serious — didn't matter. It was like Marcus thought he was perfect.

Then, as swift was my anger came, it melted away when a realization popped into my head: he wasn't worth it. Marcus wasn't worth the pain or the suffering, or the agonizing twinge I felt in my chest every time I imagined his naked body pressed against Debbie's. I was only twenty. I didn't have to waste my love or my life on this shit-bag. I was choosing to ride the Marcus train, but I could get off whenever I wanted to. As I stared at his handsome face, I sensibly decided I wasn't going to ride any longer.

With a loud sigh, I held up my hands, causing him to face me once more. "Marcus, I'm going to say this loud and clear, so you get it through your thick head. I do not want to be with you anymore. I am breaking up with you, and there is nothing you can do or say to change my mind."

Marcus raised his brows skeptically. "Is that so?" He smirked and took a step toward me, his brown eyes dancing with mischief. "Do you really think you can just forget about me, Lily? Forget about everything we shared together?"

"Yes," I replied confidently. "I believe I can."

With a large grin on his face, Marcus kept advancing until he stood only a foot away from me. Before I had a chance to withdraw, he reached out and wrapped his arms around my body. I gasped from surprise and squirmed against him.

"Let me go, Marcus!"

He ignored my plea and dipped his head towards my ear. "Tell me you feel nothing," he whispered silkily, and brought his lips against mine.

My eyes widened with surprise when Marcus stuck his tongue inside my mouth, twirling it against my own. His kisses were rough, sloppy — and not all that great. When he finished tonguing me, he lifted his head happily, as if pleased with himself for forcing his mouth on me.

I glared at him and wiped my lips with the back of my hand. "Was that the best you could do?" I asked him arrogantly.

Marcus ignored my insult and replied, "Let's go back to my place, Lily. I'll show you the best."

After rolling my eyes at him, I shoved his shoulder. "That's all you care about, isn't it? Getting laid."

"If I recall correctly, you enjoyed it when I was on top of you," he stated slyly.

I laughed and backed away. "I was faking it at least eighty percent of the time."

"Oh, please," he replied with a laugh. "You love my sex."

"Not as much as Debbie does, I'm sure."

As soon as the words passed by my lips, Marcus' devious expression vanished off his face. "Stop bringing her up, Lily," he instructed icily.

"No, Marcus. I won't stop," I told him with a frown. "I'll never stop. Don't you understand?"

"So, that's it then? It's over?"

I nodded. "Yes, I'm afraid so."

"What if I can't accept it?"

"Either you accept our breakup ..." I began with a shrug. "Or I get a restraining order. It's really up to you, Marcus."

Marcus glared at me, obviously disliking those options. "You would really do that to me, Lily?"

"If you don't leave me alone, I'll have no other choice."

He slicked a hand through his dark brown hair. "Fine. If you can just throw away our love—"

"I didn't throw away anything, Marcus. You did," I told him fiercely. "You fucked up. Not me."

"Whatever," he replied, waving his hand arrogantly. "I'm sick of fighting with you about this."

"So am I." I folded my arms and added, "Now, if you'll excuse me, I have a call to make."

I turned my back to him and pulled out my cell, dialing my home number. I took a few steps away from Marcus, and kept my voice low when I answered my father's questions. I didn't want Marcus eavesdropping on my conversation.

"Lily, thank God. I was worried about you!" my father said when he picked up. "I almost drove down to Sam's to check up on you."

"Sorry, Dad. I had to ... deal with something."

"Did you call a tow-truck?"

"No, I didn't call a tow-truck, Dad," I replied with a sigh.

"Oh, okay. Well, am I picking you up?" he asked.

I twisted my head slowly, and my gaze flickered over at Marcus, who was watching me intently. I had a feeling he would still be standing there until my dad came and picked me up. As much as I just wanted him to drive over here, I knew if my father found Marcus hanging around me, he would flip out.

A few weeks ago, I had made a promise to my dad that I would stop seeing

Marcus — but I had blatantly lied to his face. I had kept dating him behind his back, up until this very moment. Now that my relationship with Marcus was over, I did not want my father finding out that I had disobeyed him. The punishment was the least of my worries; I just did not want him to be disappointed in me.

Therefore, as my father's concerned voice buzzed in my ear, I sighed and closed my eyes, realizing I had to think of some way to dissuade him from coming to pick me up.

"Lily, are you still there?" Dad asked me worriedly. "Hello?"

"Yes, I'm here," I said, turning around to face Marcus. "But, uh ... I'm just going to walk home, okay? It's only a few blocks—"

"Nonsense," my father replied quickly. "I'll come pick you up."

"It's all right, Dad. I'll be fine. Don't worry about me."

"Lilianna, what is the matter with you? Has something happened? You're acting very strange."

I winced and bit my lip. I hated lying to my parents — especially to my dad, but I had no other choice. He couldn't find out about Marcus.

"Nothing is wrong, Dad. I just don't want to bother you. It's past midnight, and you have work in the morning. Besides, the house isn't that far away from Sam's — and I've walked the route plenty of times before."

There was silence on the line before my father inquired, "Are you sure, Lily? There's no other reason why you don't want me coming over there?"

"Yes, I'm sure," I said firmly, trying to sound confident. "I'm okay."

"All right ..." he sighed. "If anything happens to you on your way, though, call me as soon as possible."

"Of course, Dad. See you in a bit," I
told him softly.

"Goodbye, Lily."

I closed the phone and placed it inside
my purse once more.

"What was that all about?" Marcus
asked me curiously. "Something's wrong
with your car?"

I wasn't surprised in the least that he
had been listening. "It won't start," I replied
irritably.

"But you're not really going to walk
home are you, Lil?"

I nodded and looked off down the dark
street, ignoring the odd, troubled feeling in
my chest. "Yes, I am."

"It's too dangerous," Marcus replied.
"Let me drive you home."

"It is not dangerous," I told him,
reaching for my car keys. "I've walked home
after midnight plenty of times before. I'll be
fine." I pointed the keys at my car and

pressed the automatic lock button. When the car beeped that it was locked, I pocketed the keys.

"Don't be so stubborn, Lily," he said.

I rolled my eyes and glared at him. "I'll be whatever I want, Marcus. It's none of your concern anymore."

Without waving or even saying goodbye, I headed for the end of the parking lot. Marcus ran after me — just as I assumed he would — and begged me to reconsider his offer. He even tried to bribe me with a milkshake if I got into the car with him. A milkshake, really? That was the best he could do? How old was I? Five?

I ignored his offer, and when he tried to grab at me to prevent me from leaving, I took off running, refusing to glance back as I hurried down Jessup Street.

"Lily, come back here!" Marcus shouted at me, but I ignored him and kept running, wanting nothing more than to get as far away from him as I possibly could. A satisfied sensation came over me as I realized I was starting a new chapter of my life, one which did not involve Marcus Brantley.

Chapter Five

It was super chilly outside — but that was New Hampshire for you. I should've been used to the cold weather; I'd lived there all my life, after all. I wrapped my bare arms around my body for comfort, hoping to give myself some warmth. I cursed my stupidity for not grabbing my jacket from the backseat of the car. I'd been walking for nearly ten minutes since leaving Sam's, and I was starting to rethink the idea. Maybe riding home with Marcus would not have been so bad ... at least I wouldn't have felt completely alone.

The streets were pitch black; the streetlamps provided the only light, and it seemed as if they were stationed a mile apart. A lot of the houses I passed had their porch lights turned off, and so I wandered the streets in complete darkness, trying to keep my mind from thinking terrifying thoughts — which was very hard for me to do. As much as I tried to fight them, I kept imagining a lunatic jumping out at me from behind a bush. *Not helpful thinking, Lily.*

When I crossed onto Gallavan Street, an odd wind blew directly past me and down the sidewalk. I watched curiously as it picked up various leaves and debris, twirling them high into the air ahead of me. Then, all of a sudden, the wind stopped — and the leaves fell straight down onto the cement. I froze in mid-step, wondering why that had happened. *I'm not educated on wind patterns or anything, but I'm pretty sure that's not normal wind behavior.*

I kept on walking though, trying to ignore the danger I felt in the pit of my stomach. I just couldn't shake the feeling that something awful was about to happen, and as soon as I saw Lockless Woods, that feeling intensified. I stared wide-eyed into the dark forest, searching for ... well, I'm not exactly sure what I was searching for. I just had a feeling that someone — no, *something* —was hiding amongst the trees.

Then I heard it. That familiar, menacing voice calling to me.

"Lilianna ... "

My heart leapt into my throat, and I staggered as fright took control of my legs. I backed away from the woods warily, praying to God that I was imagining the voice. *Of course! That must be it. It's just my imagination working overtime.* There was nobody—

"Come to me, Lilianna ... "

Then the wind returned, but this time it came blustering toward me, at a force so powerful it knocked me backwards onto the road. I gasped as I fell, my pulse pounding rapidly. Once the shock wore off, my butt burned with pain from the fall, but I disregarded the ache. I had more important things to worry about — like running away.

Without a moment's hesitation, I jumped to my feet and hurried from the woods. I ran all the way across the street, turning hastily on to Meryl Lane. I didn't glance behind me as I ran; I was afraid that if I did, I would find somebody chasing after me.

When I neared the four-way stop, only two blocks away from my house, a large figure was standing in the middle of the street, directly underneath the traffic light, about thirty feet away from me. Massive for a man, the person was somewhat hunched, with its arms spread slightly at its sides. The stranger's rigid stance frightened me, and I was afraid to move — afraid to even breathe. Then, the figure morphed, and my jaw dropped when I noticed the large spiraling horns jutting out of its head.

"No way," I breathed, and took a

cautious step backwards. Flashes of my nightmare exploded in my memory, and I gasped when the monster's name involuntarily rolled off my tongue.

"Darcamius," I whispered.

Once I realized what I'd said, I slapped my hands over my mouth, shaking with fright. A few seconds passed and nothing happened. The figure still stood there, staring at me. I trembled, awaiting its move.

After squeezing my hands into fists to give me strength, I called out, "What do you want?"

Finally, the figure moved. I watched, horrified, as the stranger lifted its right arm and pointed directly at me. It seemed as if time stood still while I stared slack-jawed at the mysterious creature. I didn't know what to do — how I was going to get away. Then, in the blink of my eye, it sprinted towards me.

I screamed, turning around running

toward Lockless Woods, figuring it was my only chance at escaping. I knew those woods like the back of my hand. Even though it was dark, I was sure I could lose the creature within those tall trees. With a deep breath to calm my throbbing heart, I plunged into the forest.

I ran and ran, keeping my eyes fixed on my immediate surroundings. The deeper I trekked inside the woods, the darker it grew. The only light I could count on was from the moon above — but the clouds were inconsiderate of my need, and kept hiding it. I pulled out my phone with shaky hands and tried to use it as a flashlight, holding it out in front of me as I ran, and it surprisingly helped me a ton. I avoided a few large bushes I would not have seen without it.

At about a quarter of a mile inside the woods, I realized I was nearing Lisa Wagner's old tree fort. I'd visited this part of the woods many times with my girlfriends in junior high. I hoped that if I climbed up the fort before the monster had a chance to spot me, I might stand a chance. The height would give me an advantage, and he might not even look for me up there.

With a rush of determination, I ran faster, yearning to reach the tree fort before the demon found me. I recognized a large tree stump when I ran past it, and I knew I was getting close. It wouldn't be much longer now; the fort was only a few dozen feet away.

"I can do this," I whispered confidently.

When I spotted the white rickety house sitting high up in the trees, I smiled. It was like a sanctuary in this dark forest, and I couldn't contain my glee. I was so ecstatic that I hurried towards it carelessly, overlooking a large tree root that jutted out of the ground. My foot got caught and I fell, smashing my knee and my forehead into the dirt. I groaned, my eyes tearing up at the pain.

My knee burned, but I suppressed the further urge to moan by biting down on my tongue. Knowing the monster was somewhere nearby, I tried to stand up — but the pain was much too great. I lay back down onto the ground, my forehead pounding and my sight growing foggy. This was it ... the end. As I lay there in silence, I wondered if the demon truly meant what he had said in my dream. He couldn't have though, right? It was too disgusting for me to even fathom.

My breathing turned jagged when I overheard the sound of footsteps crunching against the forest floor — and heading straight towards me. I braced myself, feeling completely overwhelmed with fear when the footsteps stopped directly behind me. I tried to get a look at the monster, but

I was too weak and gave up. Then, a pair of hands grabbed me and hoisted me into the air. I struggled to remain calm, but I found that it was useless. I knew I was goner.

As the stranger cradled my body in his arms, I glanced up at his face, frowning when I noticed my sight was still hazy. I couldn't make out who it was that held me; their features were a blurry mess. I gasped, feeling my body growing limp — darkness beginning to eat at the corners of my eyes.

"Don't worry, Lilianna. You're safe now."

It was the last thing I heard before everything went black.

Chapter Six

The strong scent of burning wood drifted up my nostrils, startling me from sleep. When I opened my eyes, I found myself sitting in the middle of a forest in front of a makeshift fire, all alone. My memory was foggy. The last thing I remembered was arguing with Marcus in the parking lot. I couldn't remember why I was loafing around in the woods, but I knew I had to get out of there ... I had to get home. When I tried to stand up, however, that's when I realized my hands were tied.

My eyes widened as I stared down at the heavy rope binding my hands. I tried to wriggle them loose, but it was too thick and wouldn't budge, and its coarse texture began to irritate my skin. Panic struck me when I remembered I had been walking home — but I hadn't made it — the strange figure standing in the road ... it had horns ...

That's when my memory kick started. My pulse quickened when I realized I was a demon's captive. The most terrifying scenarios ran through my mind, and I couldn't help but imagine the worst. What was he going to do with me?

Suddenly, I heard movement to the left, a low shuffling sound coming from some tall bushes only a few feet away. Fear crept up my throat as I awaited my kidnapper. My eyes watered at the thought of dying, and I hung my head, praying to whoever was listening to spare my life. I was too young to die — I had my whole life ahead of me.

A twig snapped on the ground in front of me, and I gasped. I lifted my head to stare at the towering stranger, my eyes growing wide as I studied his face. Realization struck me, and I cowered, knowing who he was. Shoulder-length straight black hair, olive skin and bizarre grey eyes ... it was the same man who'd visited the coffee shop earlier — the shape-shifting beast from my nightmare.

"Oh my God ..." I murmured, completely trembling with fear. Flashes of my nightmare burst in my mind, and that's when I began to really freak out.

"You ... you're that demon! You were at Unique Java ..."

The man said nothing. He turned away, walked around the fire pit, and sat on a fallen log on the other side of the fire, facing me. After he sat down, he dropped two plastic bags on the ground near his feet. My heartbeat quickened at the sight of them. What were in those bags? Weapons? Chemicals? Was he going to chop my body into little bits and tote me around in them?

My captor rolled his grey eyes, as if he knew what I was thinking, and lifted one of the bags upside down, emptying its contents. Relief washed over me as I stared at the various packages of chips and cookies. He'd brought me food? What for? Why was he going to feed me if he was just going to kill me? It didn't make any sense. I glanced back at the demon, growing anxious when I noticed he was watching me closely.

"What am I doing out here?" I asked him, hoping he wouldn't get angry if I asked him questions. "What do you want with me?"

He still said nothing, and picked up a large stick on the ground and began poking the fire. I watched him to do this for a few minutes, hoping he was going to say something — tell me why he had kidnapped me. However, when he tossed the stick to the side, and glanced over at me, he still didn't respond to my question.

"Are you going to kill me?" I asked

him, breaking the silence.

The demon's head shot up and he glared at me; his intense eyes made me tremble. He looked furious for a moment, but the expression passed when he tossed the stick to the ground.

"No," he replied, his soft voice chilling me to the bone. "I'm not going to kill you, Lilianna."

I raised one brow, skeptical of his admission. "I don't understand? If you're not going to kill me, then why did you bring me out here — in the middle of nowhere? What do you want with me?" My voice cracked due to my frazzled emotions, and I closed my eyes, fighting the tears that were threatening to spill.

"I know you must have many questions," the demon replied slowly. "Questions that you need answers to. I will tell you all you need to know in due time, Lily. But for now, let's just sit here in peace."

I opened my mouth to speak, but I realized it would do no good. He was putting up a brick wall, and the only thing I could do was what he said. I sighed then, simply giving up, and glanced down at the colorful packages of junk food near his feet. My stomach rumbled with hunger just from the sight of the snacks. I couldn't help it — I hadn't eaten anything since my lunch break at work.

After gesturing to a bag of chips with my head, I asked, "May I eat something please?"

He didn't seem annoyed at my request when he swiftly picked up the bag and stood. My brows rose with surprise after he reached down to remove a can of my favorite soda from the other plastic bag. How did he know what I liked to eat? When he joined my side, he knelt down in front of me and popped the top off of the soda. The demon lifted it to my lips, but I turned my head swiftly to the left, feeling awkward at the idea of him feeding me.

"Do you want to eat or not?"

Refusing to glance at him, I replied, "Yes, but not that way."

"Well, what do you suggest?"

I turned my head, facing him once more. His face was only a few inches from mine, and for a split second I got lost in his pretty grey eyes. They were different — unlike any I had seen before. Cool silver, with flecks of gunmetal grey. It was unreal that anyone could possess such lovely-colored eyes. Then again, he was a demon. It was unreal that he even existed.

Uncomfortable from his heavy stare, I bowed my head before saying, "I'm perfectly capable of feeding myself. Just untie my hands."

The demon shook his head and smirked. "Typical."

"What's that supposed to mean?" I asked hotly.

"You're typical," he replied simply, before rising, and I wondered what he meant by that.

With a sigh, the demon reached inside the right pocket of his dark-grey trench coat to remove a small Swiss Army Knife. I flinched at the sight of the knife, wary when he bent down in front of me once more.

His grey eyes studied me as he flipped the knife out and said, "Listen to me very closely, Lily. If I cut this rope and let you eat like a human being, it would be unwise for you to insult my generosity by running away from me." With a flash of his eyes, he moved to cut my binds — but not before he whispered, "Because if you do run away, I will find you ... and bring you back here."

My breath got caught in my throat when he sliced through the thick rope in one swift movement. It unraveled from my hands and fell to the ground, and I breathed a sigh of relief as I rotated my wrists. It felt so good to be able to move my hands around freely once more. The demon offered me the bag of chips and soda before standing up and walking back over to his log.

I grinned as I popped a chip into my mouth, enjoying its salty taste. I realized it was one of my favorite kinds of chips too. After taking a swig of the soda, I peeked over at the demon. I was surprised to find him not staring at me for once. He was actually gazing up at the night sky — a sort of tranquil look in his eyes. I glanced up at the stars too, finding a breathtaking view. There were so many stars in the sky — much more than I had seen in my entire life, more than I had ever seen from my balcony at night.

Suddenly, everything felt somewhat familiar. The stars, the woods ... it was as if this moment had already happened before. I knew that couldn't have been possible. It was a strange feeling nonetheless, uncomforting, and when my eyes passed over the demon, I found he had returned to watching me again, but now he was wearing a glum expression. I wondered why.

"There are many things you aren't aware of, Lilianna," he said suddenly, startling me. "Things that will haunt you for the rest of your life."

I propped my chin up in the palm of my hand and watched him from across the campfire. The firelight danced across his face, almost hypnotizing me. He was so very handsome — and unique, in a way that enchanted me. But he didn't always look this way. I had to remind myself that he was a demon. He was evil, pure and simple. This handsome man was wearing a mask, and I knew what he truly was.

I toyed with idea of escaping, but I

knew there would be no use in trying. If my kidnapper was indeed a demon, then he was faster than me — stronger too, and I would never be able to outrun him. I was stuck with this otherworldly stranger, and I had no choice but to do what he said. If I didn't obey his orders, I feared the consequences.

All of a sudden, he frowned at me and said, "I'm not going to hurt you."

I rolled my eyes and crossed my arms. "And I'm just supposed to believe that? Give me a fucking break. You kidnapped me!"

The demon shook his head and replied, "I know waking up in the middle of the forest with me as your company must be unsettling—"

"Unsettling? Are you insane?" I shot back, my temper catching us both off guard. "I'm hanging out in the woods with a ... I don't even know what you are! Unsettling doesn't even begin to cover it!"

"I am deeply sorry for putting you in this predicament, Lilianna, but I'm afraid I had no other choice. Just a few more minutes in those woods and he would've—" His voice broke off, and my captor stared back at the sky. He sighed before finishing, "He would've taken you."

"Who?" I asked eagerly. "Who the hell are you talking about?"

Lowering his head to glance back at me, he frowned and replied, "Never mind, Lily."

"No. Don't do that! Tell me what is going on. I have a right to know!" I told him fiercely. "It's the least you could do."

After a few moments of thinking it over, he finally spoke. "I didn't want to delve into all of this tonight, Lilianna."

"Why not?"

"Because I wanted to spare you from the truth for as long as I could." His voice sounded sad, and it caught me off guard.

Why was he acting so concerned about me?

"If it'll help me understand—"

"Yes, it will help you understand ....
but it will also terrify you to the brink of
insanity. This horrible truth may cause you
to do the unthinkable. It's happened
before."

"Before?" I mouth incredulously. What
did he mean by *before?*

"Yes," he replied softly. "To the
woman you represent."

My jaw dropped. "What does that even
mean?"

His grey eyes softened as he said,
"You're a reincarnation, Lily — of a very
important woman ... who's the reason for
this entire mess."

I watched him warily, confused by his
admission. Me, a reincarnation? I didn't
believe in that sort of thing, so I didn't know
how to respond. How could I be a
reincarnation? I was Catholic, not Buddhist.

"It doesn't matter what religion you are, Lilianna. Reincarnation is a cycle that has been with us since the dawn of man. Every single person is reincarnated."

How did he do that? How did he know what I was thinking?

He sighed then, studying me closely. "I can read your thoughts, Lily. I hear everything."

I frowned, finding it difficult to process. "Excuse me? What?"

"I have the ability to read a person's mind."

"No way," I replied shortly. "Nobody — not even a demon would be able to do that."

"It's true," he said softly. "I've been reading your thoughts this entire conversation."

"I don't believe it ..." I said with a frown, and shook my head. *So he can read my mind, eh? Well let him try.* I thought of something bizarre — something nobody would even dream of thinking. Not a number, a color — or even a place. When I had the perfect thing in mind, I smiled, feeling confident I would prove him wrong.

I said smugly, "Okay. If you've got this so called ability, what am I thinking of right now?"

He exhaled loudly, obviously annoyed with the idea that he had to prove himself to me. "You're imagining a grizzly bear riding around on a unicycle juggling three yellow bowling pins." With another sigh, he added, "Now it's on a motorcycle ... wearing a pink tutu ... juggling fruit." The demon slid off his the log to lean his back against it instead, and then lifted his arms above his head with triumphant smile, seemingly pleased he had proved me wrong.

"Satisfied?" He asked me with a charming smirk.

I blew a long piece of hair out of my

eyes before crossing my arms and accepting defeat. "Fine," I replied coolly. "You can read minds."

"Thank you. Your faith means a lot to me," he responded with a wink.

Glancing away from his smug expression, I studied the area around me, wondering which forest I was currently residing in. It couldn't be one in Jackson County. I knew this demon was too smart to light a fire in woods where there was a heavy population — or to keep me close to home. He had traveled far ... and I had a feeling it was somewhere very secluded.

"We're still in New Hampshire — but near the border and close to Maine," he told me, earning my attention once more.

"I see," I replied softly, staring down at my feet.

"And just for the record, I'm not the same demon from your nightmare. I know that's what you immediately assumed because of our similarities, but it's not true. I am not Darcamius."

My head snapped up and I stared over at him curiously. "You're not?" I asked with a whisper. "But I thought—?"

He shook his head. "No. I'm not."

"Then who are you?" I blurted loudly, scooting up straight.

I was baffled by his admission, and honestly didn't know whether to believe him or not. He possessed the same eyes, hair, and facial structure as Darcamius. Although ... that was just the demon's front — he actually looked like a rabid beast with spiraling horns. Did this mystery man before me have a different form as well?

The demon stood up swiftly, and with the slight bow of his head, introduced himself. "I am Septhim Ananias, but you may call me Seth."

"Seth? Well, that's a rather odd nickname for a demon. It's a—"

"Human name? Yes, I know," Seth interrupted, sitting back down in front of the fire. "My mother gave me the name Seth when I was born — and my last name too. It's Greek."

"Your mother?" I mouthed, confused. "I don't understand. How can you have a Greek last name if you're not—?"

"That's because I am," he interrupted again.

"You're what?" I breathed.

"Human," Seth replied simply. When I gave him a skeptical look, he added, "Well, partly."

Partly? If he was telling me that his mother was a Greek woman, then his father must have been a demon. That must mean he was a ...

My jaw dropped from shock, and I glanced over at him hastily, unable to say the baffling thought.

Seth's grey eyes watched me closely

from across the fire. They flashed when he whispered, "Yes, Lily. I'm a half-demon."

Chapter Seven

"A half-demon?" I repeated incredulously.

Seth nodded, eyeing my reaction closely. "Yes."

"Wow," I muttered, absolutely taken aback.

I recalled Darcamius' evil voice from my dream, his desire for me to have his child. Maybe it was possible ... but it was still so bizarre to even consider! I had never believed in demons or anything of the paranormal, so it was hard for me to take in all this with a straight face.

"So ..." I began slowly, dragging a hand through my dark hair. "If your mother was a human, then your father is obviously a demon. Who is your—?"

My voice fell as I looked him over,

realization knocking the breath out of me. The hair, the eyes ... of course! Why hadn't I realize it sooner? Darcamius was Seth's father!

I muttered my theory with a slight squeak. "Darcamius is your father?"

Seth said nothing in return, and continued to watch me, his grey eyes alert.

How could that be? What if this whole time we've been sitting here, he was just biding time, waiting for Darcamius to show up? The idea sent chills of fear down my back.

Now skeptical of Seth's motives, I asked, "If Darcamius is your father, then why are your helping me? What's in it for you?"

With an annoyed grunt, Seth settled himself comfortably on the ground. "Just because Darcamius is my father, doesn't mean I'm anything like him. We may share blood, but that's as far as our resemblance goes," he replied firmly.

"Well, you sure look like him," I retorted.

"Looks aren't the same as morality, Lily," he shot back.

I folded my arms and asked, "Okay, so why don't you agree with your father, hm? What's he done? Besides being a scary, evil creature, I mean."

"I don't agree with his ways of living, or his conquest of filling the mortal realm with half-demons," Seth replied icily. "But, for the most part, I cannot forgive him for torturing my mother and forcing me into her life."

I grew silent and reached for my bags of chips. He stared blankly at me, as if he wasn't going to disclose his past. After a few moments of awkward silence between the two of us, Seth finally budged.

"I was born in the spring of 1601 in Arta, Greece," he began, a smile forming on

117

his face as if he was remembering his early years.

"1601?" I almost choked on my chips. "1601? No way. That means you're ..." I frowned, trying to do the math quickly in my head.

"Over four hundred years old."

My brown eyes widened from surprise. Four hundred years old? He couldn't be! Seth looked just a few years older than me.

"No way!" I exclaimed.

"Way," Seth grinned.

"If you're four hundred, how come you look the way you do?"

"What, handsome?" Seth asked me with a smirk.

I rolled my eyes at his dull joke and said, "Be serious. Why don't you look old and worn out?"

Seth's amused expression withered as he replied, "A demon's lifespan is significantly longer than a human's. Since I am a half-demon, I age, but at a much slower pace. Full-blooded demons can actually live an infinite number of years. Darcamius himself is five thousand years old."

"Five thousand?" I stammered in amazement. "Five thousand?"

"Yes ... and he's not the oldest."

"Jesus. So, if he's five thousand, will you reach that same age one day too?"

"Yes. I most likely will — if I live my life in solitary."

His remark confused me. "Why does that matter?"

Seth snorted at my question. "Say I buy a home somewhere and live there for forty some years. When I don't age, people are going to notice. It would only be a matter of time before somebody finds out that I'm not just their friendly neighbor — but an inhuman abomination. They would be at my front door with torches and pitchforks. It has happened to my kind many times."

"Oh," I replied softly.

What Seth said was cruel ... but it was also true. If word got out that he was a demon, then people would stop at nothing to rid him from the world. No one would understand him — they wouldn't care if a part of him was human. The only thing a scared person would see was his demonic half. Honestly, it was kind of hard to see past that detail.

"I'm very sorry," I whispered, and I meant it sincerely.

I could see that Seth was heartbroken from the reality of his life, and I found myself wanting to know more about him. He seemed so different than his father, and I realized that I wasn't scared of him like I was Darcamius. I know I should've been — him being a half-demon and whatnot — but I simply wasn't. Seth wasn't frightening or menacing at all. He was ... kind of nice for a kidnapper.

"Tell me about your mother, Seth," I implored with a smile.

And to my surprise, Seth actually began to tell me his story.

"My mother was a slave in a rich official's house. She was a very beautiful Greek woman — so my father would always say — desired by most men who came in contact with her. Even her owner tried to force her into an affair — but my mother wouldn't have it. She was a very righteous woman and refused to be the object of any man's desire."

Seth frowned and shook his head before adding, "Until Darcamius entered her life and gave her no choice but to succumb to him."

"What did he do to her?" I asked him.

His grey eyes turned black as he said, "He charmed my mother — tricked her into his bed. When he showed her his true self, she tried to get away ... but it was no use. Darcamius raped her, then left her alone and pregnant on the basement floor of her owner's home. When word got out she was with child and not married, she was whipped and ridiculed. It was not permissible for a woman in that time to be promiscuous."

I cringed, saddened by his mother's hardships, and I wondered how she had dealt with her unwanted pregnancy — and the fact that an unholy creature had raped her.

"What happened to your mother, Seth?"

My question caused him to flinch. "She died a few hours after giving birth to me. All she left me was my name. Nobody wanted me when I was born, and it wasn't until I was teenager, when Darcamius came to collect me, that I realized I had any family."

"What about your mother's family? Didn't they take you when she died?" I asked hastily.

Seth shook his head and replied coldly, "No."

"What?" My eyes began watering at his response. "How could they abandon you like that?"

"I'm a half-demon, Lilianna. Remember?" Seth said heatedly, stabbing the logs in the fire violently with the stick. "Why would anyone want me?"

"But someone must've looked after you?" I asked him eagerly. "You were just an infant!"

He nodded. "Someone did take me in. But it wasn't until I was older that I realized they were just like me."

"A half-demon?"

"Yes. His name was Antonio Vigoss, and he had abilities unlike any half-demon I've ever known. His power was almost as great as a full-demon's."

"Was he good too? Like you are, Seth?"

"Good?" Seth repeated, smiling faintly at my remark. He seemed pleased that I considered him honorable.

"Well ... you are, aren't you?" I inquired hastily, hoping I wasn't wrong.

With a swift nod, Seth replied, "I am ... but it's hard to say if my old friend was. Antonio would damn the race of men with a swig of a stiff drink, then save some poor soul's life the next day. I can't really say for certain if he was good, but I considered him to be. There are only a few half-demons who will associate with humans at all."

"How come?"

Seth sighed and cracked his neck. "Most half-demons spend their entire lives trying to appease the full-blooded ones. Like my brother Aleneas, for instance. No matter how many times they beat him down or scar his body, he will always yearn to be accepted. But they will never recognize him as one of them. He knows this, and yet still he tries. He's a fool."

Brother? Seth had a brother?

"Yes, Lilianna. I have many siblings," Seth said abruptly, peeking at me from the corner of his eye.

"Are they all half-demons?"

I felt sort of annoying asking him all these questions, but it was making me feel better. If we focused on him, then we wouldn't have to talk about me — and how Darcamius had been chasing me through Lockless Woods only hours before. Or the fact that he wanted to mate with me. I needed to keep my mind off of my impending fate, if only for a little while.

"Not all of them are half-demons, no. I have a few full-demon siblings. Though, they would tell you otherwise."

"They don't like you?" I didn't need

him to answer that question. I could tell by the fury etched on his face that it was true.

"No. I'm just pond scum to the likes of them."

My heart went out to Seth. He seemed so angered by his demonic ties, as if he resented them. If I were in his shoes I'm sure I would too, but then again, I didn't know what having heightened abilities felt like. Perhaps Seth enjoyed being a demon way more than he was letting on.

I said his name softly, barely above the tone of a whisper. "Seth?"

"Yes, Lily?"

I bit my lip warily before asking, "Do you like being half-human, half-demon?"

He raised his brows at my question and frowned. "Do I like being a mixed breed? Have you even been listening to my ramblings for the last thirty minutes?" Then Seth frowned and asked, "What do you think, Lilianna?"

With a shrug, I replied, "I don't know, Seth. I mean, it sounds awful to have to move around a lot and never settle down somewhere — and to have people fear you all your life. But you have telepathic powers ... and you can actually read my mind! That's an amazing ability."

Seth stood before saying, "A few meaningless traits that I would trade in a heartbeat just for a chance to be a normal human being."

I stared up at him and smirked. "So you would trade everything that makes you great just to be weak like me?"

He shook his head swiftly and replied, "Not weak. Beautiful and flawed. Completely vulnerable and capable of so many wonderful emotions."

"Yeah. Weak," I retorted with a laugh.

"I guess we'll just have to agree to disagree," Seth said with a deep exhale.

I grinned at him. "I guess so."

Then our conversation dawdled to an end, and an uncomfortable silence befell us. We both sat there quietly, Seth staring at the sky and me gazing at the fire-pit. A cold chill struck me suddenly and I stuck my hands out towards the fire, enjoying the way the heat from the flames eased away the numbness in my fingertips.

For some odd reason, I couldn't tear my eyes away from the fire, the way it twisted and turned, viciously eating a new log Seth had thrown inside the pit only moments before. It was beautiful to me — until I recalled my nightmare, the flames spreading over my body. I shuddered at the memory and glanced at Seth, finding him studying me once again.

"Why do you always stare at me?" I asked him with an aggravated sigh. It was kind of creepy how he kept watching me — like he couldn't take his eyes off of me or something. Marcus had never done that, and he claimed to be in love with me.

Seth shrugged nonchalantly and replied, "I'm just watching you," and he said it as if it wasn't a big deal.

"I know that. " I replied with exasperation, puffing my bangs out of my eyes.

"I'm asking you why!"

"To make sure nothing happens to you — whether it's of your own volition or Darcamius'."

I rolled my eyes. "Right."

Seth ignored my rude gesture and said, "I think it would be a good idea if you tried to get some sleep now, Lily. We've got a big day ahead of us."

"Where are we going?"

"Some place my father will never find us."

"And where is that exactly?" I inquired curiously.

Seth's grey eyes flashed, and he

seemed annoyed that I was so inquisitive. "It's for me to know and for you to find out tomorrow. Now, lie down and get some sleep."

"What if Darcamius finds us?"

"He won't."

"How can you be so sure?"

With a frown, Seth replied, "You just have to trust me, Lily. I won't let anything happen to you."

"Right. I'm just supposed to trust my demon kidnapper to keep me safe from another demon who also wants to kidnap me. Don't you think that request is a little bizarre, Seth?"

Seth didn't seem amused. "Just go to sleep ... or would you prefer I make you?"

I said nothing. I followed orders like a good girl and lay my head on the ground. As I tried to get comfortable, a slight breeze caressed me, and when I rubbed my arms for warmth, Seth's grey coat fell around my body. I glanced up at him, surprised but thankful for his gesture, feeling uneasy about the intense look in his eyes. We stared at each other for some time, neither of saying a word, until he moved away and returned to his usual spot on the other side of the pit.

"Good night, Lilianna," he told me softly.

"Good night, Seth," I replied, watching as he settled back against the log.

I stared at him from across the fire, an odd sensation of peace grabbing hold of me. Here we were, stranded in the middle of a forest at night, out in the open among wild animals and mutant-sized insects, but oddly I wasn't scared. Normally I would've been hyperventilating at the thought of a wolf or bear approaching me while I slept, but for some reason I knew I was going to be okay. Although I wasn't sold on the idea that I could trust this half-demon, there was undoubted belief in the back of my mind that Seth would protect me throughout the night, and it gave me the security to fall into a sound sleep.

Chapter Eight

Seth woke me at dawn by shaking my shoulder and complaining about the need to be on our way. I yawned and rubbed at my eyes, feeling too tired to move, but I couldn't ignore his annoying badgering for long. With a loud yawn, I sat up, and as I did, a sharp twinge shot through my back. I doubled over in pain, realizing it was probably caused by the poor sleeping arrangement from last night. I guess I had slept on the wrong side of the forest.

"Are you all right, Lilianna?" Seth asked me concernedly.

I nodded and pressed at the tense muscles in my lower back. "Yeah, I'm okay. My back just hurts."

"Ah," he replied, and helped me onto my feet.

Without asking, Seth walked around me and lifted my shirt to place his hands flat on my back. He then began to knead at my shoulder blades, his fingers digging into the hard muscles, startling me stiff.

"Seth, what are you doing?" I asked him uneasily, trying to ignore the pleasurable sensation.

"We won't get anywhere if you're in pain. Besides, I don't want to listen to you whine about your back the entire journey there."

My eyes narrowed at his statement. "Hey! I do not whine!"

"Sure you don't," Seth replied with a smirk.

He rubbed my shoulders next, kneading at the muscles closest to my neck. This spot usually sent me into a daze. Whenever I went to a massage therapist and they worked that area, I drooled like a dog. But when Seth touched me, I experienced a different sensation, like his hands were radiating heat, sending a rush of tingles and warmth all over my body. I closed my eyes and sighed deeply. His hands were so strong — unlike any I had previously encountered before. As I stood there helplessly, my mind began to wander, imagining his hands on other places of my body.

Then my face heated up and my heart started pounding with embarrassment, frightened by my rash imagination. I shrugged out of Seth's grasp quickly and moved away, taking a deep breath to steady my pulsing heart. I couldn't face him until I was back to normal. When the desire had melted away from my thoughts and my face was no longer flushed, I turned around and forced a smile — hoping he wouldn't suspect anything.

Seth looked confused — almost wounded — as if he was afraid he had done something wrong. "Lily, if I offended you—"

"No," I said hastily, raising my hand to stop him. "You didn't. I really appreciate you trying to help me, Seth. And I'm fine, really."

Seth didn't seem convinced. "Are you sure? If you're upset, you can tell me."

I shook my head. "I'm not, honestly. It just felt ... weird."

Without hesitation, I went to crack my back. My eyes went wide with fear when I remembered it was sore, and after I cursed myself for being so stupid, I awaited the pain. However, there was no pain. Surprisingly, the pain was gone. I grinned happily, twisting and turning my back left and right with ease. He had actually fixed it.

I smiled at Seth and said, "My back feels much better! Thank you."

"Already? I only massaged your muscles for a minute or two."

"Yeah, but you have great hands," I

told him, and my cheeks turned pink at the memory of his touch.

Seth smiled slightly before moving away and wandering over towards the plastic bags on the ground. There was another bag that I hadn't noticed before sitting on the far side of the log. He lifted all of the bags into his arms before motioning for me to join him. I grabbed my purse and his coat off the ground and walked towards his side of the fire pit.

"It's time to leave," he said firmly, studying me closely.

"Are you going to tell me where we're going now?" I asked.

"You'll see soon enough."

I shrugged and decided to let it go. There was no use in pestering him; I knew he wasn't going to tell me even if I asked till I was blue in the face.

Seth seemed relieved that I decided to leave it alone. His usual, tense expression melted away as he said, "All right then. Hold still."

In a flash, he wrapped me up in his arms, holding me as he would a small child or infant. I frowned, feeling uncomfortable by being held such a way — especially by him. No one had carried me like that in a very long time, and it felt somewhat unnatural.

"What are you doing? Put me down!" I demanded anxiously.

Seth shook his head. "We need to get to the cabin as fast as we possibly can — before Darcamius finds us. I cannot let you move at your own pace. It'll only slow us down."

"How long is he going to keep looking for me?" I breathed, fear creeping up my throat when I recalled the previous night's events, remembering Darcamius standing in the middle of the street and pointing directly at me. I almost choked on that same fear when I recalled the demon lord's menacing horns.

"As long as you live, Lilianna, he will always be hunting for you," Seth replied. "Darcamius will never stop until he finishes what he started all those years ago."

"But Seth ..." I began, uneasily.

"There's no time for arguing, Lily," Seth said sternly. "We must get out of this forest. Now, hold onto me tight and brace yourself. You might be a little overwhelmed."

"Overwhelmed? Why—" I closed my mouth in shock as Seth began to run — at a speed so fast I was shoved back against his chest from the force. The forest whirled past me, and I shut my eyes for fear I would vomit. I clung to Seth's body, mentally praying for him to slow down. I knew he wanted to get to wherever we were going, but my head was starting to throb from the intensity of the speed.

He was running exceptionally fast. I was shocked that it was even possible to move at such a pace. Was this speed his usual tempo? He was a demon after all, and when I opened one eye to glance up at him, I was surprised to find that the speed did not affect him whatsoever. Seth actually seemed thrilled as he darted past trees; I even thought I saw a slight smile on his face.

After a few minutes of demon-sprinting through the woods, Seth's speed dropped considerably to that of a dull jog. I breathed a sigh of relief and glanced around eagerly, expecting to find myself in a different atmosphere. To my surprise, we were still surrounded by a gazillion trees. I frowned and crossed my arms, disappointed.

"What gives?" I asked him irritably. "I thought you were taking me out of the woods?"

"I never said that," Seth replied,

before coming to stop. He dropped me carefully on to my feet and added, "I said we needed to get out of *those* woods."

"Ugh," I grumbled, sighing as I rubbed at my pounding head. Great, now I had a headache too. Could this day get any worse? I glanced back at Seth's blank expression and my frown deepened. "So what now?"

"We continue the rest of the way on foot."

His directive confused me. "I thought you said I was too slow?"

"You are. But I thought you might enjoy traveling more on your own two feet."

My jaw dropped from surprise. "But what about Darcamius? You said—"

"Don't worry, Lily," Seth interrupted. "He's not nearby. If I sensed him, we would still be running."

I took that as a good sign and smiled. Grateful to be standing on the ground once more, I said, "Thank you for doing this, Seth. I was getting a little sick from how fast you were running."

"I know," he replied. "Your thoughts were driving me crazy."

Without another word on the matter, Seth resumed walking. I followed closely behind him, making sure I wouldn't fall behind and get lost — but I had a feeling Seth wouldn't let that happen. As we journeyed further into the uncharted wilderness, I realized that the forest we now roamed was considerably different from the previous one.

There was much more plant life among this forest floor, and I even detected a few berry bushes and patches of flowers. My eyes fell upon a small area of maroon flowers that looked similar to daisies, only with more petals. They were very pretty, and an irresistible urge to pluck one filled my thoughts. However, when I went to pick a flower, Seth grabbed my hand.

"I wouldn't do that if I were you," he said, eyeing me closely.

"Why not?" I asked incredulously. "It's just a little flower ..."

Seth smirked at my reply. "It's poisonous. Just one touch and you'll contract a rash. You will be itching your hand for days."

I frowned at him and rolled my eyes. "What? Just from this pretty flower?"

"Yes. And if you were to eat it, well, let's just say you wouldn't be in the greatest of moods." He let go of my hand to add, "Trust me, Lily. Don't touch the flower."

"Fine," I grumbled, and with a huff, I gave up and left the flower alone.

We continued on our journey in silence, until the sound of rushing water filled my ears. I grinned and hunted for the source. I searched all around, but I couldn't find a river or lake or anything nearby. After vivaciously searching, I decided to simply ask Seth where the source of the sound was; he would know. Being a demon, I'm sure he had super acute senses.

"Seth, where's that sound coming from?" I asked him suddenly, trying to quicken my pace to keep in stride with him.

"The Swift River," Seth replied, casting a short glance over his shoulder.

"Is it nearby?" I inquired eagerly.

"Yes ... and no," he said, twisting his head back around.

I folded my arms in annoyance and asked, "What does that even mean?"

"It means that yes it's nearby, but no we are not going to go find it."

"Seth, come on!" I exhaled. "Can we please go see the river?"

Staring straight ahead, Seth responded firmly, "No."

"How come?"

Seth laughed and peeked over his

shoulder to look at me. "You ask a lot of questions, Lilianna. Are you always this inquisitive when you don't get what you want?"

"I wouldn't know," I responded with a frown. "I always get what I want."

"I'm sorry, but that privileged lifestyle of yours is going to change."

I glared at the back of his dark head and muttered, "I'm getting the feeling."

"Don't worry," Seth said. "I know you're not looking forward to all of these changes in your life, and I can't promise that you'll enjoy your stay with me. All I can promise you is that you will be safe. Darcamius is not going to hurt you again, Lily. I swear it."

Seth's promise was just empty words to me, and as much as I wanted to believe them, I couldn't. I followed behind him the rest of the way in silence, wondering if I should trust him with my life. I barely knew

145

him, and he was a half-demon after all. He could've been lying to my face this whole time, all the while leading me to my doom. *I should've tried to run away when I had the chance.*

On our way, we passed a cave and a hot springs, Seth having to practically drag me away from them. There were so many beautiful, captivating places inside these woods — I couldn't help but be interested. Although, I had a strong feeling in my gut that Seth wasn't going to give me a chance to experience any of them.

Then, without warning, Seth came to an abrupt halt, and I wasn't paying attention and slammed directly into his back.

"Ouch," I groaned, trying to ignore the pain in my aching nose. "What'd you do that for?" I asked him angrily.

"We're here," he replied, turning to give me a slight smile.

"Huh?" I glanced over his shoulder

curiously to find a wooden cabin nestled in a clearing just a few feet ahead. I took a step towards it slowly, hoping that Seth was joking. "This is it?" I asked him incredulously, staring uneasily at the small aged cabin that stood before us. "He must be kidding ..." I muttered.

Seth said nothing, and wandered towards the front door. I watched him leave with a frown, anger and disappointment settling in the pit of my stomach. Of all the places in the world, this is where we end up? He couldn't honestly expect me to stay cooped up here — in this tiny shack in the middle of the forest. It looked like a dump.

With a twist of his head, he motioned for me to join him at the door. "Come on," he said keenly. "I'll show you the inside."

"Eh." I obeyed sullenly, and joined him at the front door. Seth opened it swiftly and held it open for me to pass through first.

The interior of the cabin wasn't much

of an improvement from the exterior. The walls were bare panels of dark wood with four small windows, two in the kitchen and one on both sides of a fireplace. There was an oversized blue couch sitting in the middle of the room facing the fireplace, which was decorated with a few small trinkets: picture frames, figurines, and a small hourglass. None of the pictures in the frames were of Seth, just aged photographs of an older couple.

The kitchen was on the far side of the cabin, near the hallway. It was very quaint, with red and blue checkered curtains covering the top half of the windows. There was a small wooden table sitting in front of the windows, with four darker wooden chairs tucked under each side of the table. Thankfully, there was a sink, a refrigerator, and a stove.

"Where's the television?" I asked Seth shakily, frantically searching for the set.

Even an old TV would do, just as long as there was one. I didn't even care if I had to watch programs in black and white.

"There isn't one here," he replied, trekking deeper into the cabin.

"Oh my God," I moaned, depression hitting me cruelly. "I'm going to die of boredom."

"Come on, Lily. It's not that bad."

"Not that bad?" I breathed. "Not that bad? Are you 'freakin' serious? What am I supposed to do out here for entertainment? Living in this rundown cabin with you is one thing, but I'll suffer without some television, Seth."

He rolled his grey eyes, disregarding my complaint as he beckoned me towards the hallway. Then a thought crossed my mind. "Wait. How does a place like this even have electricity?" I asked. "It's in the middle of nowhere, and there aren't any power lines out here."

"The cabin runs on a generator. I have to keep refilling the fuel every few months or so. I've never had a problem with electricity here."

"Oh. Well, that makes sense." I glanced about the room once more, and I sucked in a deep breath when I noticed there wasn't a phone in the cabin either. Of course there wasn't. Having contact with the outside world was the last thing a kidnapper wanted. My heart dropped when I realized I wouldn't be able to get in touch with my family, and the idea that my parents would never know I was alive and well killed me.

"Follow me now," he said solemnly. "I'll show you to your bedroom."

"This little shack has bedrooms? I'm surprised. I thought I was going to have to sleep on the ground again."

Seth ignored my dig and continued walking, leading me down the cabin's short hallway. I noticed there were three doors in the hall, each painted a different color. The middle door was bright blue and wide open, exposing the small blue bathroom behind it; the other doors were yellow and burgundy, and both were closed.

He directed me towards the right side of the hall, where the burgundy door stared back at us. There was a large flower etched into the middle of the panel. I lifted my hands to trace the etching, surprisingly intrigued by it. As I felt along the rigid lines in the wooden door, I had an undoubted feeling that this was the door to my room.

"Do you like the flower?" Seth asked, watching me closely.

"Yes," I replied softly, still studying its intricate detail.

"It was carved into this door many, many years ago."

I peeked over at Seth curiously, detecting sentiment in his tone. "Did you do this?"

Seth smiled at me and shook his head. "No. Alas, I am not a very good artist."

"Then who did?"

"An old friend of mine," Seth whispered. He stepped closer towards the door, smiling slightly as he placed a palm against the smooth grain. "The door was already in place, and he stood here in this very spot when he carved the flower. I remember watching him — being surprised at how skilled he was."

I was taken aback by Seth's changed mood. "Tell me about him, Seth," I implored.

He glanced back at me and frowned, his sentiment melting away. "Perhaps I will ... but another time."

Seth reached his hand out to open the door, and the door creaked as it swung open, revealing a lovely little bedroom. My eyes went wide with amazement — surprised by the simplicity and beauty of the room. It was a small space, but just right, with a tall mahogany wardrobe sitting against the left side of the room, and a four-poster bed arranged against the right wall. There was a yellow quilt covering the mattress, with tiny pink flowers embroidered into the fabric.

I couldn't help but smile as I entered the enchanting bedroom, wandering over towards an antique floor mirror I'd overlooked. Without hesitation I touched the old frame, my fingertips grazing over more flower carvings. Flowers seemed to be this room's theme, and I had a feeling that it had belonged to a woman once upon a time.

After studying my reflection in the mirror for a second or so, I turned away and glanced down at a small table sitting near the dresser, shocked to find a pile of clothes sitting neatly atop it. I reached for the garment on top of the pile and aired it out.

It was a maroon blouse, my size, and looked similar to a shirt I already owned.

My eyes flickered back at Seth, wondering how he knew to buy me the right clothing. Same with the chips. Had he honestly been watching me my whole life like he'd said? It couldn't be true. I would've noticed him — how could I have not? He was very out of the ordinary.

Seth spoke suddenly, bowing out of the bedroom. "I'll leave you to get situated. I will call for you when I begin making dinner."

"Okay," I replied, watching as he smiled and shut the door behind him.

When the coast was clear, I sighed in despair and settled down on the corner of the bed. My mind kept reeling with one thought: was I really being forced to live here in this cabin with a half-demon? When silence answered me, I knew the sad truth.

"I have no choice," I whispered, lying

154

down on the bed.

It was true. I had no choice. Seth wouldn't let me leave, and if I did, his father would take me instead. I was bunking with the lesser of two evils, sure, but I still wasn't certain I could trust Seth. I didn't know much about him except that his father was evil and that he had a human mother. He could be just as bad as his dad — worse even. By agreeing to come with him I could've gotten myself into a really bad situation.

However, when I imagined Seth as a danger, something odd happened. It was like those worried feelings were wiped clean from my mind. I couldn't bring myself to account him as a villain; something inside my soul assured me he was good. I couldn't put my finger on exactly what that feeling was, I just knew it to be true. Seth would never hurt me.

That assumption gave me comfort,

and I was able to retreat from my slump. I slid off of the bed and began making the bedroom more to my liking, angling furniture and dusting off shelves and tabletops. I kept my thoughts fixed on the positive. The happier I was, the easier it would be to suffer through this nightmare. Once it was over, I could go home.

Chapter Nine

"Lilianna, may I come in?" Seth asked, with a knock at my bedroom door.

I closed my antique wardrobe and glanced over at the closed door. I'd been tidying up and rearranging my room for the last hour. Seth had cleverly left me alone to myself. I was thankful to him for giving me space; I needed the time to think and get used to my new surroundings. Sure, I liked my bedroom, but I was beginning to feel homesick. How in the world was I going to get along without my family and friends? It'd only been a day and already I missed them terribly.

With a soft sigh, I moved around the bed and stepped closer towards the bedroom door. "You can come in, Seth," I told him.

He opened the door slowly, as if afraid he was intruding. "I'm sorry for interrupting you, but I'm about to begin cooking a stew and I was wondering if you would like to give me a hand with it?"

"Sure thing," I said with a nod, and joined him in the doorway. "I'm done rearranging anyway."

Before we walked down the hall and out into the kitchen, Seth asked, "Do you like your room, Lily?" He studied me closely, and I knew my opinion was important to him.

I gave him a genuine smile and replied, "Yes, Seth. It's lovely."

He returned the smile and said, "Good. I'm glad."

Seth led me out towards the kitchen. A large metal pot was resting on one of the stove's burners. He pointed to an arrangement of vegetables spread out on the kitchen table, along with a large knife and a hunk of red meat sitting on a wooden cutting board. I eyed the knife nervously, a spark of fear grabbing hold of me. Seth's voice snapped me out of it though.

"You can start on the carrots," Seth told me eagerly, pointing towards them. "I'll take care of the meat."

"What is it?" I asked him, studying the meat closely. I hoped it wasn't something cute like a deer or fox.

"I don't want to say," he told me with a smile.

My brows rose with alarm. "Why not?"

"You might not want to eat it if I do."

I frowned at his warning and reached for a raw carrot. "Never mind then."

We worked on the stew in silence, Seth slicing the meat and me cutting up the vegetables. After the preparations were done, we dumped all of the ingredients in the large pot and covered it. Seth said it would take about thirty to forty minutes before the stew would be edible, and so we sat down at the kitchen table and waited.

Seth being the charmer that he was, decided to bring up the most unpleasant subject — a subject I was still trying to forget.

"Have you had any nightmares recently, Lily?" Seth asked suddenly, shattering the quiet.

My stomach lurched and my heart started to race. I couldn't help but get all worked up whenever I started thinking about that horrid nightmare. Whenever I even tried to recount what happened, it consumed me. I wasn't in the mood to talk about Darcamius or anything "demon related," but I had a feeling that Seth wasn't going to drop the issue.

"Yes. I've had one."

His grey eyes flashed with worry. "When? Was it last night?" he inquired hastily, leaning forward on his chair.

"No," I replied, wondering why he was acting on-edge. "It was the other night ... the night before I met you."

Seth eased back into his chair. "Oh, all right then."

"Why does it matter?" I asked. "So what if I had a nightmare? It's not that big of a deal. Sure it freaked me out, but—"

"Do you think that nightmare was just a coincidence? That you just happened to dream of the same demon that's been after you for centuries?"

I shrugged, not fully comprehending where he was going with that. "I don't know, Seth. Was it?"

Seth's grey eyes narrowed at me. "No, Lilianna. It wasn't."

"What do you mean it wasn't a dream? Of course it was! It wasn't real!" He didn't agree with me, which only scared me more, and I whispered, "Seth, I don't understand."

"I know, Lilianna," he said then, and

161

scratched his dark head. "What was the nightmare about?"

I rubbed at my neck, avoiding Seth's watchful gaze. "It was about him."

Seth grew antsy once more. "What happened, Lily? You must tell me everything."

I nodded and closed my eyes; the memory of the dream still fresh in my mind. Never before could I recall a dream so vividly. I knew this nightmare would be forever etched into my soul; I would remember it until the day I died.

"I was in a dark place. I don't really know where, but I knew I was alone. Then, suddenly, there was a fire and Darcamius emerged from its flames. He called to me — wanted me to join him inside the inferno. I wouldn't go ... even though he was so alluring."

"What happened next?"

Seth's voice seemed a thousand miles

away as I placed myself back in the dream with Darcamius. I kept my eyes closed, the nightmare so lucid and real. I gasped when I remembered the demon lord holding me against my will, caressing my skin with his hands. The memory made me shudder with disgust.

"He grabbed me, and I tried to get away but I couldn't move. I was frozen. Then I saw … what he was … and I was so scared. Darcamius told me he wanted me to have his child, and that he would be back for me. He vanished, and then the fire—"

I gasped softly, my eyes snapping open as the memory of the fire sweeping over my body filled my head. I was shaking, my eyes tearing up at the corners. Seth stared at me from across the table, darkened with rage. He stood up his chair swiftly, and walked over to me.

He placed a gentle hand on my shoulder and said, "It's going to be okay,

Lily. He's never going to hurt you again."

I smiled up at Seth, grateful to him for being so kind. How could the spawn of such evil be so generous and compassionate? I wiped at my eyes and tried to calm down, but Seth's earlier statement still bothered me.

"Seth, why did you say it wasn't a nightmare?" I asked, slightly afraid to learn the truth.

He sighed and shook his head, then walked back over to the other side of the table. After sitting down, Seth said, "I'm sorry, Lily. I shouldn't have said it like that. Yes, technically it was a nightmare, but some elements of the dream were real."

"What? How can that be?" My hands were wringing the hem of my shirt.

"Darcamius wanted to see you — and he did, just not in what you humans would call real time."

"Huh?" I wasn't going pretend like I

had any idea what Seth was talking about. The fact that Darcamius had actually visited in my dreams was hard enough to grasp.

"The dream realm is an actual place, Lily. Humans don't consider it "real," and therefore they close their mind to it. Demons, however, have harnessed the ability of traveling there and can visit whenever they choose. In fact, most demons do most of their chaos in the dream realm."

I frowned at him and replied, "You're telling me that when people dream, they actually go somewhere?"

"Yes and no. They don't physically, but their subconscious does. Except nowadays, most humans can't even make it out of the gate."

"Gate?" I felt like my brain was on overload. First I came face to face with a demon, and had to deal with the fact that they do exist. Now Seth was explaining that there's a dream realm where demons torment humans while they sleep? I guess I finally understood the saying: *Ignorance is bliss.*

"I'm sorry for dumping all of this on you, Lily," Seth told me. "I didn't want to upset you, but I think if you know the truth, it'll benefit you in the long run."

I glared at him, feeling overwhelmed by all of this frightening information. Seth expected too much of me. I was only twenty! I couldn't deal with all of this madness. I missed my simple life — when I thought Marcus cheating on me was the worst possible thing. All of this ... it was just too much. Then, before I knew what I was doing, I jumped out of my chair, anger flaring in my chest.

"Forgive me if I don't agree with you, Seth. I know you're just trying to help me, but in the last twenty four hours I've had to accept the idea that demons are real and that one is after me. I'm holed up in a rickety cabin in the middle of nowhere with you — a half-demon — far away from my friends, family, and civilization. I'm stressed out, exhausted, and scared to death that your father is going to violate me in ways that I don't even want to think about! I just need a little time to myself ... to come to terms with this horrible situation that I now find myself in."

Seth seemed offended by my outburst, but he nodded and replied, "I understand, Lily. I apologize. I shouldn't have asked you about your nightmare."

I rubbed at my temples, which were beginning to ache, and quickly replied, "I need to be alone for a while, Seth. Excuse me.

Before he had a chance to reply, I raced out of the kitchen and down the hall, the reality of my situation pounding down on me. I held in my tears before I made it to my door, but after it was closed they came rushing down. I threw my body onto my bed and wept for the tragedy that was my life. Nothing would ever be the same again, and I had a feeling I would never be the simple girl I used to be before that first nightmare.

Chapter Ten

Time passed slowly for me while in Seth's care. There wasn't a calendar on hand in the cabin. To keep track of the days I wrote them down on a small piece of scratch paper I found in one of the drawers. Sixteen days and counting, confined to this tiny structure. I was surprised that it was only so few; it felt like an eternity.

I wasn't allowed to step foot outside the cabin, and there wasn't much for me to do except cook, clean, or read — and Seth wasn't very good company. Ever since that first day in the cabin he had kept his distance from me. The only time I saw him was during the evening when we prepared dinner together. Most afternoons he was gone, always running off without an explanation as to why, and I hated him for leaving me by myself.

I tried my best to get him to talk to me, but he always brushed me off or changed the subject; it was obvious to me that he was hurt. For some reason, the way I reacted had really got to him. I felt bad about the whole ordeal, but I didn't know how to apologize without sounding immature, and so I eventually decided to try a different tactic: to kill him with kindness.

When he returned home for supper, with a plump canvas bag slung over his shoulder, I greeted him at the door. He seemed surprised to see me waiting for him, bright-eyed and happy that he was home. Seth opened his mouth to greet me at first, but he decided against it and instead nodded at me and walked on by, heading for the kitchen. I followed after him, planning on forming a conversation with him. No matter how hard he tried to evade me, Seth wasn't going to leave me to myself any longer.

Without a word, he dropped the canvas bag on the kitchen table, emptying its contents. I watched him attentively as he placed a carton of milk in the fridge, along with containers of grapes and strawberries. Thank God he wasn't making me pick our berries in the woods like some barbarian.

"So, where'd you go?" I asked him enthusiastically, hoping he would detect my interested tone.

Seth glanced over at me and frowned, my question apparently bothering him. "I had to go get supplies. We were running low on milk."

After folding the bag and tucking it away in one of the cabinet drawers, he turned away from me and wandered towards the hallway. My heart stung with guilt when I realized he was trying to avoid me, but I followed after him. I was not going to let him duck the situation any

171

longer.

"You've been gone for quite a while, Seth ..." I replied, following him to his room. "You're always gone."

He paused in his open doorway and turned his head to the side, not giving me a clear view of his face, but just enough so I could see the pain in his eyes. "Why do you care? I'm just a half-demon who's holding you against your will. You don't care if I come or go."

I bit my lip, my face heating up from embarrassment. "That's not true. I—"

"Isn't it?" Seth snapped, spinning around to glare at me. "You've made it very clear, Lilianna that you don't want to be here. But if I hadn't —" He voice dropped and he shook his head suddenly. "Never mind."

"No," I replied, taking a step towards him. "Please finish what you were going to say."

He stared at me; his features set in stone. "If I hadn't risked my life to protect you by intervening — you'd be dead, or worse!"

"I know," I whispered, my eyes falling to the floor from shame. Seth was right. If it hadn't been for him, I would've been impregnated with demon spawn.

"No, I don't think you've fully grasped the situation, Lily. You may understand that I saved you, but you still hate it here."

"I don't—"

"Please don't lie to me, Lilianna," Seth responded grimly. "I can read your thoughts. There's no use in lying."

I pursed my lips, accepting defeat. He was right. There was no way I could hide anything from him; it was tough living with a mind reader.

"I understand the reason for your hatred," he continued. "But this cabin is your safe haven. Here, you're completely protected from Darcamius' wrath."

I frowned and replied, "Why here though? Out of all the places in the world, why this cabin?"

"Because this cabin is dear to me. It holds many memories, and it's the only place I've kept hidden from my father all these years. He has never found it … and he never will."

"How are you managing that?" I inquired.

Seth sighed and shook his head. "That's not important. All you have to know is that I'm trying to help you, and all I ask of you in return is to respect that — and me."

"I do, Seth," I said, meeting his assertive gaze. "I'm just overwhelmed by all of this. It's a lot to take in at once, you know?"

He nodded. "I do. You've handled it pretty well though, compared to the others."

"Well, it wasn't easy. I'm still expecting

to wake up and find myself back home in my bed."

Seth smiled slightly and replied, "I'm sorry, Lilianna. I wish that was the truth."

I smiled back at him, relieved that we were finally talking again. Those two weeks of solitude had killed me. I didn't know how long I was going to be cooped up in this cabin, but I knew I would rather spend my time with this demon than alone.

"Seth, do you mind if I ask you a question?"

He shrugged. "What is it?"

"I want to know about the others — the other women Darcamius sought after." When he didn't reply, I bit my lip gently and asked, "Will you tell me about them? Please?"

Seth's eyes grew dark at my request, and I wondered if he was angry at me. But his gloomy stare eased away when he replied, "Sure, Lily. I'll be glad to tell you."

"Their names were Ysmay, Louisa, and Carrine."

We were sitting at the kitchen table, Seth's locked hands resting neatly on the tabletop. I was picking raw strawberries out of a bowl, chewing thoughtfully as I learned about the women I was reincarnated after. It was all so interesting. I wondered if they had looked like me or if we all had similar personalities. I doubted Seth would know about that though. He was a man after all — well, partly.

"Louisa and Carrine were born at least a century apart. Ysmay's and Louisa's years were spread farther, considering that Ysmay was born in 1014."

"Whoa," I almost choked on that information. "That was such a long time ago."

Seth nodded. "She lived through a very difficult time-period. I'm not sure if you know much about the first millennium, Lily, but life was hard on women. It was hard on men too, but especially on the women."

"No, unfortunately I don't know much about history. I wasn't a big history buff."

"Well, I'll spare you the gruesome details, but a woman's duty was not effortless. I don't know much about Ysmay, though. She was before my time. I do know that she was a field worker — and very beautiful. Her beauty and virtuousness drew Darcamius. A woman so lovely yet so pure was rare to come by. He couldn't resist Ysmay ... and his desire to fill the mortal realm with his spawn was birthed."

"Really? It all started with her?"

"My father has been intrigued by humans for as long as they've existed. He explained that his interest was purely in having power over humans; however, when he found Ysmay, his desire for power spiraled out of control and turned into an obsession. When Ysmay died, he found

177

other unwilling women to bear his spawn, but it was never enough. He could never forget Ysmay — and no matter how many half-demons were birthed, he could not let her go."

"What happened to her, Seth?" I whispered sadly.

Seth frowned at me and replied, "Ysmay was doomed for being a pure soul. She never stood a chance against Darcamius' wrath. He raped her, and not knowing his own strength, killed her, leaving her dead in the field where she worked."

That information cut deep into my heart. My eyes went wide from shock and I found I was close to tears. "I can't even imagine...." My voice broke, and I took a deep breath. We sat in silence awhile after that, me trying to come to terms with Ysmay's horrid fate, while Seth sat quietly, watching me. I was afraid to ask Seth about the others, but I knew I didn't have a choice. No matter what happened to them, I had to know about Louisa and Carrine.

"Louisa was the first reincarnation, right?" I said suddenly, breaking the heavy silence.

Seth studied me closely before saying, "Yes."

"How come so many years passed before Ysmay was reincarnated?" I asked him curiously. "But Louisa and Carrine were born a hundred years apart?"

"Reincarnation is unpredictable. You don't choose when you're reincarnated — it simply happens. The soul of that deceased person must first find peace to move on, before it can settle into the body of another. Ysmay suffered a horrendous death at the hands of my father. It's no wonder her soul lingered in the afterlife for such a long period."

"Oh ..." I muttered, shaking my head. "That poor woman."

Seth frowned at my glum tone and said, "Perhaps we shouldn't jump into all of this tonight, Lilianna. You're obviously upset over what I told you about Ysmay."

I shook my head sternly and said, "No. I'm fine. It makes me want to vomit, sure, but I'm okay. I want to know about the others. No, I *need* to know."

"Lily, I don't—"

"Please, Seth," I interrupted, my eyes flashing with impatience.

With a sigh, Seth said, "All right, Lilianna, if you insist. Louisa was born in 1799, almost two hundred years after I was born. Her mother abandoned her at a convent, and Louisa grew up to become one of the sisters — a nun if you will."

"Really?"

"Yes. And like Ysmay, Louisa was a kind and virtuous woman. She never hurt a soul — physically or by word of mouth. I had the pleasure of knowing her for a short while."

"How did she die?" I asked him weakly, hoping her death was less vicious than Ysmay's.

Seth stiffened, and he brought a hand to the bridge of his nose, pinching it tightly, his eyes locked on the surface of the table. "Louisa was safe from Darcamius for years because of her upbringing. The convent was a holy place — Darcamius and his minions could never enter it. I warned her about him, once I learned of my father's plans to burn down the convent. She was greatly disturbed by the news." His voice fell and he closed his eyes, the memory apparently causing him great pain.

"Seth? Are you okay?" I reached my hand across the table and gave his shoulder a reassuring rub. "You don't have to talk about it if you don't want to."

"No, I must. You need to know," Seth replied firmly. "It's important that you

181

understand the pain Darcamius inflicted on these women. If we're not careful, he could do the same to you, Lily."

"What do you mean, *if we're not careful?*"

"Darcamius has ways of luring humans. He has many powerful abilities, as you well know, some of which mesmerize and control. It's how he got his hands on Carrine. He was clever, and by manipulating her mind he almost succeeded."

"Oh ..." I replied softly, shuddering at the thought of falling for one of Darcamius' tricks. "Is that how Louisa died?"

Seth shook his head solemnly. "No," he said. The painful look on his face returning. "The night my father was to burn down the convent, Louisa evacuated all the sisters and priests in residence, and thanks to my warning, no one was injured that night — except for Louisa."

"Seth, what did Darcamius do to her?"

"He didn't get the chance to hurt Louisa. During the chaos, he tried to collect her, but she wouldn't go with him willingly. I was pushing my way through the crowd when Darcamius advanced towards her. I watched in horror as she took a knife from the folds of her dress and slit her own throat. There was nothing I could do to save her ... she had lost too much blood. Louisa died in my arms that night, and that's when I vowed to protect her next incarnation. I would not allow another woman to fall prey to my father's wrath."

"That's awful ..." I whispered, choking up over Louisa's desperate act.

"The worst part is that Louisa took her own life — she will be forever damned. And it's on account of my father. He ruined her."

I frowned at the sight of Seth's distress. "I'm so sorry, Seth."

"I curse myself every day for not moving quicker — not fighting harder through those crowds. Perhaps if I had, Louisa would not have killed herself. Maybe she would have lived."

"You can't blame yourself, Seth. It's Darcamius who is to blame for these tragedies. He killed those girls. Not you."

Seth forced a smile at me before replying, "Thank you, Lily, for your kind words, but I can't agree with that statement. I was weak, and I cost those women their lives — Louisa and Carrine. I should have protected them from my father, but I failed them both ... their blood is on my hands."

I sighed, frustrated that I couldn't get through to him. No matter what I said, I knew well enough to leave it alone; he wasn't going to believe anything I said anyhow.

"Will you tell me about Carrine?" I asked him softly.

He nodded. "Of course. Carrine was ...

an interesting girl. Born in 1920s, she was unlike Louisa and Ysmay in almost every way. She was wild, exciting, and turned heads everywhere she went. Carrine was a beauty — the kind that kept men on their toes. But although she had a vastly differently nature, there was one thing she shared with the others."

"What was that?" I inquired.

Seth smiled, gazing off as if he was remembering her. "Kindness. I came to Carrine's rescue when Darcamius cornered her in a dark alleyway in Chicago. The year was 1940, and it was hardly suitable for a young woman to be walking around downtown alone. Carrine didn't care though — she had a gun on her person just in case trouble arose, which she pointed directly at my face when I tried to rescue her, but I digress. I had been trailing Carrine all evening, from night-club to night-club. I kept close, but she never knew I was there.

"A jazz band was playing on the stage, and I looked off for a mere moment, but that was all my father needed to lure her out of the club and into the cold night. I tracked her scent to an alley a few blocks away, where I found Darcamius forcing himself on her. I intervened swiftly, stunning him to say the least, and flew off with her kicking and screaming."

"You ... flew away with her?" I asked incredulously.

"Yes," Seth replied simply.

"That couldn't have been easy," I laughed.

He grinned at me and shook his head. "No. Carrine was flailing around the entire time — and I almost dropped her twice."

"Where did you take her? Here to the cabin?"

"No, I didn't wind up at this place 'til long after Carrine's death. I took her to an abandoned mansion in Pennsylvania.

Thankfully it was fully furnished, and out of town a ways. We stayed cooped up there for many nights ... before my father tracked us."

I bit my lip, my heart pounding with dismal suspense. "Couldn't you hide her from him?"

"I tried my best, but it wasn't enough. My powers weren't as developed as they are now — at least, I didn't know how to use them to my benefit."

"So he took her away from you then?"

Seth's eyebrows narrowed at my question. "Darcamius set fire to the mansion, and Carrine got trapped inside the master bedroom on the second floor. I left her alone to battle him outside, and before I knew what he'd done, the entire structure had ignited from the flames of his hands."

"Why would he set the house on fire if he knew she was still inside? Was he trying to kill her?"

"He didn't intentionally. Darcamius sent in one of his demons to recover Carrine beforehand, but she escaped and fled upstairs. The entire lower level was aflame in a matter of seconds — but the demon still pursued her. She ran to her bedroom and hid under the bed. He searched and searched for her, but the fire was too savage. It engulfed the building, trapping her and Darcamius' minion inside it."

"Oh my God! She was burned alive?"

He nodded grimly. "I heard Carrine's screams as the fire consumed her and the mansion, but I could do nothing to save her. I tried to fight my way past Darcamius, but by the time I stunned him and got free, there was nothing but fallen debris and ash where the mansion once stood. Carrine was gone ... and with her went my father's chance at an heir."

"Jesus ... that's so sad."

My heart ached for those women —

the poor souls Darcamius sought to corrupt. I couldn't help but to think that Ysmay and all of her reincarnations were cursed, which meant I too was cursed. I was next in line. What horrid fate would befall me? Would I be burned alive? Perhaps I would follow in Louisa's footsteps and take my life before Darcamius had the chance to.

"You mustn't think that way, Lily," Seth told me softly.

"How can I not? Your father is hunting me, Seth. It's obvious he won't stop until he finds me."

Seth nodded. "It's only a matter of time before he starts looking for you himself, but as long as we remain here in this cabin — within the barrier — we're safe."

"Barrier?" I repeated the word slowly, confusion setting in.

His eyes darkened, a displeased expression crossing his face. So that's why the cabin was a "safe haven." Seth was using his powers to hide it from Darcamius. I found this information mind-blowing. There had been some sort of invisible barrier around me this entire time and I didn't even know it? How bizarre.

"How does it work?" I asked him curiously.

He hesitated at first, but eventually replied, "The barrier works as more than just a shield. It completely erases the cabin's existence from other demons. If my father were to show up here, in this exact location, to his eye the cabin would be invisible. There would be nothing but empty woods for him to scan."

"But he could still feel us, right? Our aura or whatever?"

"No. The barrier also hides our presence from him, while giving off an empty sensation. Darcamius would feel almost compelled to leave as soon as he stepped foot within the barrier."

I scratched my head, all of this new information bewildering. "So, we're completely safe in here, right? He can't touch us?"

"Correct," Seth replied simply. "It took me a long while to perfect this barrier. It's not something a half-demon can usually achieve. I was lucky."

"Will this barrier always be here? Is it permanent?"

"No. If I die, the barrier disappears." Seth frowned when he noticed I was a little overwhelmed. "I'm sorry, Lilianna. I wanted to tell you, but I thought it best you didn't know the extent of my abilities."

"Did you think the information would frighten me?"

He nodded. "Yes. I did."

"Why?" I asked curiously.

"Because the others were terrified of me — of what I could do. They never told me, but I knew."

I shook my head at him and replied, "It doesn't scare me, Seth. You don't scare me … and I've gotten used to the idea of living with a demon. I've already known that you have certain abilities, so why don't you trust me with the truth?"

Seth scowled and glanced down at the table. "It's hard to trust humans. They are so fickle with their emotions and opinions that it's generally a bad idea for a demon to count on them. I knew a few demons from my past that fell in love with humans, only to be betrayed and humiliated by them."

"But I thought you liked humans?"

"I do. I prefer humans over demons, but that doesn't mean I would give myself or my trust blindly to one. Demons and humans are not meant to be mixed."

I studied his stern expression closely before asking, "Even if the demon is half-human?"

Seth's grey eyes flashed at my comment. "Yes. Even then it's not wise. Our worlds are far too different. Trust me, Lilianna. Demons are power-hungry and malicious, and humans are timid and ignorant. It will never be possible for them to coexist peacefully. It's hopeless."

"So, you just always keep to yourself then? You don't let anyone in for fear they will betray you?"

He frowned at me and replied, "For the most part, yes. There have been a few humans in my lifetime that I have befriended, but they didn't know what I was. I never let them know, for if they had, they would've turned on me. That is the sad truth."

I could hear the sorrow clinging to Seth's words as he explained his desolate life. It was obvious he wanted someone to share his life with, but since he loathed demons and was a monster in the eyes of humans, he was sadly alone. He was hurting, and there was nothing I could do for him except listen.

"I know we haven't known each other for long, Seth, but I just want you to know that I consider you a friend. And I hope you know that I will never turn on you. You're my hero after all."

Seth smiled slightly. "Thank you, Lilianna. I appreciate you saying that."

"No problem. I'm grateful for everything you've done to protect me from your father."

"It's my duty to protect you, Lily. I made a vow," he said softly.

"I know."

We both stared awkwardly at each other after that, neither of us saying another word. After a minute passed, Seth cleared his throat and stood from the table, his cheeks a slight pink shade.

"Well, I think that's enough storytelling

for one night." He bowed his head to avoid looking at me and added, "Goodnight."

I watched him wander out of the kitchen and down the hall to his room, my heart now twisted with grief after listening to him. The more I got to know Seth, the more wonderful he turned out to be. So what if he was a half-demon? I felt privileged to be his friend. I grinned when I realized there was one positive outcome from his father's madness. Seth wasn't alone anymore. I was here for him — I was on his side and always would be.

Chapter Eleven

The harsh rays of the sun beat down on me, heating my neck and face. I was working out in the fields — picking corn off of their stalks and wrapping them tightly in the white cloth slung across my shoulder. It was exceptionally hot, and the long, tan gown I wore was making me all the more uncomfortable — but I tried to ignore my discomfort and focus on the task at hand. I only had three more rows to go before I was done, so I cleaned my dirty hands on the cloth before wiping the sweat from my forehead.

As soon as I plucked another husk of corn, an odd breeze passed over me, sending a sharp chill down my back. I shivered, and accidentally dropped the husk to the ground. I sighed as I bent to pick it up, and when I dusted it off with the hem off my dress and placed it inside my cloth I noticed a figure standing at the end of my row. My pulse quickened from surprise, and when I turned to glance at the person, I found a strange man staring at me.

I called out to him — asked him what he wanted. The stranger said nothing, and began to walk slowly in my direction. I frowned and backed away, telling him to keep his distance. He ignored my demands and sprang at me. Before I realized what was happening, he had grabbed hold of my wrist and pulled me into an embrace. I struggled against his fierce grip, but he was too strong to fend off.

The stranger caressed my cheek with his warm fingertips before laying a kiss on the top of my head. I screamed, uncomforted by his unwarranted affection. His grey eyes bore into me, and I saw the lust etched in them; I knew what this stranger sought. He whispered to me then, his deep voice scarring my very soul. The strange man told me I was beautiful — that he had watched me for some time. He said he had carefully chosen me, and he was going to make me a part of something very special. The man knew my name somehow, and when he uttered it, the sound made me cry.

Then, without warning, he threw me to the ground. I screamed and kicked my legs at him as he tried to kiss my mouth. He slapped me rudely, angered by my defiance. I fell still, shocked by his heavy blow. The man mounted me with a grunt — and despite my loud protests, ripped the dress from my body. I now lay there in the dirt and grass, naked and vulnerable.

He smiled at my bare skin, and when he went to raise my legs, I watched his grey eyes turn black. I screamed at the sight of his unholy eyes — terrified. This man wasn't a man at all. My mother had been right all along. Demons truly existed. After realization set in, I wrestled with the monster and tried to get away, but he held down my arms, pinning me cruelly.

"*You'll never escape,*" he said, pressing me deeper into the earth. I cried out from the pain, but still struggled with him. The demon slapped me once more, but this time his force knocked the breath out of me. My jaw felt detached, and my pulse slowed to a dawdling rhythm. I cowered beneath the demon — unresponsive while he took away the last of my innocence.

While I lay there dying, I prayed to God to spare my soul, even if he couldn't save my body. I felt a white light caress my face instantaneously and I knew that he was listening to my prayer. The creature dug his nails into my arms, oblivious that I was near death. He howled with pleasure, and as my eyes slipped shut, the last thing I saw before my death was his devilish appearance.

I rose from my sleep with a loud gasp, trembling and sweating as the vivid images of Ysmay's death filled my head. My heart was pounding as I ripped the blankets off of my body — the white nightshirt I wore clinging to me. I gagged at the thick sweat coating me and hastily peeled the shirt off and over my head.

That nightmare — vision, or whatever the hell it was — left a bad taste in my mouth. Was that what Seth had meant by *nightmares?* If so, how many more was I going to have to suffer through? I sighed and reached for a clean nightgown in my dresser, all the while trying to soothe my flaring nerves by taking a few deep breaths. There was no way I could endure another vicious death caused by Darcamius. Ysmay's had been quite enough.

I was feeling thirsty — I'd lost a lot of

water throughout the night from sweating —
so I decided to grab a glass of water from
the kitchen. When I walked out of the
hallway and into the main room, I found
Seth sitting hunched over the kitchen table.
I tiptoed around, hoping not to alert him
when I grabbed a clean glass out of the
cupboard and removed the pitcher of water
from the fridge. He didn't even stir after I
approached him, and I was surprised to find
him in a deep sleep.

I had never witnessed Seth sleeping
before; he looked so vulnerable, and calm,
and different. I had always thought he was
good looking, but at the moment, when his
grey eyes weren't staring back at me, I
realized just how handsome he really was.
No thoughts of demons or death fluttered
through my mind. I could only focus on the
unusual emotions I felt, and the pounding of
my anxious heart.

Suddenly, Seth's eyes snapped open

and he jumped from his chair; it fell to the floor with a loud thump. He seemed frenzied as he gazed about the room, seemingly searching for someone or something. I wondered if my presence has caused him to wake.

"Seth?" I said his name with fear, shocked by the sudden change in his temperament.

He ignored me and glanced up at the ceiling, his grey eyes flashing red. "Scouts," he stated angrily, before running towards the door.

"Scouts? What?" I asked anxiously, following after him.

Seth whirled around to glance back at me; his grey eyes were set in stone. "Stay inside, Lilianna. And whatever happens, do not walk out this door!"

"Why?" I asked him nervously. "What's happening, Seth?"

"Darcamius' scouts are searching the

woods for us," he replied hastily. "I sense about three nearby."

My eyes grew wide with fright. If they found out where the cabin was, it would only be a matter of time before Darcamius came to collect me himself. That thought made me tremble with absolute fear.

Seth noticed the tense look on my face. "Don't worry, Lilianna. I don't think they've located you just yet. If they had, they would've showed up at our door by now. Remember, the barrier keeps the cabin off any demon's radar."

"Then what are they doing here?"

He rubbed at his neck and replied, "Most likely they caught a whiff our trail from days ago and are exploring all their options. Darcamius won't stand for failure. He'll kill them if they come back empty-handed."

I nodded and took a deep breath, his explanation easing my worries only a little.

203

There was still a good chance the demon scouts would find me and I would be ripped from Seth and my safe haven, and then it would be all over. I had a feeling that even as powerful as Seth was, when Darcamius showed up to take me, he would be no match for his father, and I would be doomed to give birth to demon spawn.

Craning his head towards the door, Seth's frown deepened as he said, "I must go. Stay inside and out of sight. I promise I'll be back soon."

"Be careful, Seth," I said, as he ran out of the cabin, leaving me with terrible thoughts and scenarios racing through my mind.

I wandered over towards the couch, settling down with shaky knees. I was frightened that it was all over — this whole charade. Darcamius was going to break down the front door and take me away, and my life as I knew it would be finished. That thought almost brought me to tears — but I was too frightened to cry, and so I quickly pulled the blanket down from the backside of the couch and covered myself, hoping it would help hide me from the evil that lurked out in the woods.

As I lay alone in the dark cabin, I prayed for Seth's safe return, but I had a strong belief that no matter what, he would come back to me. He'd promised he would, and he wasn't the type to break a promise. I stared at the front door, waiting for Seth to walk through it unharmed and triumphant. I'm not sure how long I waited up for him before my eyes slipped shut and I fell back to sleep.

Chapter Twelve

"Seth?" I rose from my sleep with a gasp, the memory of the night's excitement flooding my thoughts. With a nervous yawn, I jumped off of the couch, tugging the soft blanket around my shoulders as I wandered the quiet cabin, anxiously searching for Seth. My heart raced with worry when I realized he wasn't back yet.

I glanced out the window and found the sky still dark, and I figured I had only dozed off for an hour or so. That realization eased my worries a little, but I couldn't stop wigging out. Where was Seth? Why was it taking so long? *He promised he would be back soon! Did something horrible happen to him out there? What if—*

My overactive imagination was cut short by loud pounding at the cabin door. I froze, my eyes widening with fear. Oh no. Darcamius' scouts had found me. I had to hide — fast — before they found me and took me to him. My pulse raced as I turned to run down the hall to my bedroom, but I paused when Seth's stern voice hit my ears.

"Lily, it's me! Open the door."

I smiled instantaneously at the sound of his voice, and my fears melted away like butter. *He came back!* I hurried towards the door eagerly, but as I was about to unlatch the lock, I hesitated. *How did I know that was really Seth out there?*

"Lilianna, please!" He pounded on the door once more.

Thinking fast, I yelled, "If that really is you out there, Seth, then tell me what I'm thinking of right now?"

I heard a slight groan on the other end of the door and then a short pause.

"You're thinking about the flower you almost picked on our journey here. The chrysanthemum."

With a sigh of relief I unlatched the door and opened it quickly. Seth glared at me before he stumbled inside the cabin hastily, locking the door behind him. He maneuvered past me and over towards one of the chairs by the table, where he sat down with a growl. I watched him with wide eyes, shocked by the various bloodstains and wounds covering his arms and face.

"Jesus," I whispered, rushing at him. "What the hell happened to you?"

"You should see the other guys," he replied with a short laugh.

I shook my head at his remark. "It's not funny, Seth! What happened?"

"What do you think? We battled," he replied with a shrug.

"You did? What—"

He held up his hand swiftly to silence me. "Don't overreact, Lilianna. Please. I'm all right."

"How can I not? You're badly injured!" I replied angrily. "Have you seen yourself? You're covered in cuts and bruises, Seth! You look just awful."

"What? This?" He gestured to his body with a snort. "This is nothing. Trust me."

"Don't joke, Seth."

"I'm not," he responded thickly. "I'll be fine by morning."

I swallowed the lump in my throat and tried to settle down, my heart was still racing. "So what happened?" I asked him anxiously. "Did the scouts find the cabin?"

"No. They weren't even close."

"Really?" I smiled with relief.

Seth nodded at me as he lifted his torn black t-shirt over his head. After crumpling the ruined shirt into a ball, he tossed it to the ground. "Yeah. I took care of them before they reached the surrounding area."

I blushed at the sight of his torso. Even in the dim-lit cabin, his abs stuck out, and I could hardly tear my eyes off of them. When I realized I was staring, I tried to focus my attention elsewhere. The large wound on his right shoulder fit that need nicely.

"That looks awful," I told him hastily, hoping he wouldn't notice my burning cheeks when I pointed to the deep gash. "At least let me clean the dirt out of your wounds."

He began to protest. "It's not necessary, Lily—" But I was already rushing to the sink, grabbing one of the clean dishrags out of the drawer. After applying some soap and running it under warm water, I returned to the table, approaching Seth hesitantly.

I forced a smile at him and instructed him to relax. "Just lean back and let me help you."

He obeyed my orders, but his body was tense when I laid the rag gently upon his wound. Seth inhaled sharply, the soap obviously causing him a little pain.

"I'm sorry," I told him softly, before proceeding to wash his torn skin.

His grey eyes flashed, but he smiled at me and said, "I'm okay. It just stings a little."

"I bet," I replied with a laugh.

I avoided Seth's gaze while I tended to his wounds, but I could feel his eyes studying me. I couldn't read his mind, but he was probably wondering why I was being so caring.

"So what happened?" I asked him, trying to keep my mind out of the gutter while I washed his naked torso. "Where did you find the scouts?"

"I found them about four miles away from here. There were three of them, like I said, but they never stood a chance. I dropped out of the sky and picked them off one by one. Darcamius is not going to be pleased when they don't report back to him."

I bit my lip anxiously and met his hardened eyes. "You killed them?"

Seth's expression eased up as he stared back at me. "I had no choice, Lily. I did what I had to do to protect you."

I responded with a nod before tending to the rest of his injuries.

He studied me closely as I cleaned out the gash on his right side, his grey eyes drinking me in. When I finished with that wound, I went to clean a deep cut on his forearm, but Seth grabbed my hand suddenly, causing me to drop the rag onto his leg. I stared dumbly at his hand grasping mine, feeling my cheeks heat up as I tried to ignore the surprising pounding of my heart.

Gazing intently at my face, Seth asked, "Tell me the truth, Lilianna. Do I frighten you?"

Seth's question caught me off guard; I admit I was entirely focused on how tightly he was grasping my hand. I glanced back at him, shocked by the unsettling expression on his face. He seemed absolutely solemn at the thought of me fearing him.

"No, Seth. You don't frighten me," I said, sincerely.

"Are you sure?"

I smiled at him. "Yes. Like I told you earlier, I'm not afraid of you. What made you ask me such a thing?"

"Because of what I did tonight. Because I killed those demons."

I sighed and shook my head. "You killed them to protect me. That doesn't make you frightening."

"But it doesn't frighten you to know I've killed?"

"No, not really," I replied honestly. "I mean, sure, it shocks me to hear you say that you did, but I know you were only acting in self-defense. You're one of the good guys, Seth. I trust you."

My answer seemed to satisfy him and finally he let go of my hand, settling back against his chair. I finished tending to his wounds in silence, and when I was done I found myself yawning. I blushed when I noticed him studying me; I must've looked like a mess.

"Go to bed, Lily. You're exhausted," Seth instructed, waving me off.

I happily obeyed his order and stood, eager to fall down on my bed, which was way more comfortable than the couch. My back was aching from laying on it for only a few hours. Why anyone would want such an uncomfortable piece of furniture was beyond me. It wasn't even appealing to look at.

When I moved away from the table, Seth stopped me to say, "Thank you for taking care of me tonight, Lilianna. I appreciate all you have done for me."

I twisted my head around to smile at him, my cheeks burning from seeing the content expression on his face, and the knowledge that I was the reason it was there.

"It's no problem, Seth. I was happy to do it," I responded softly.

He returned the smile and waved me off once more. "You need your sleep. Go."

I laughed and wandered down the hall, hurrying toward my bedroom door. After I tucked myself in and got as comfortable as I could, I closed my eyes and drifted off. Not once did I think of Ysmay's horrid death — all I could think of was the way Seth had looked at me while he held my hand.

Chapter Thirteen

The next week passed by agonizingly slow. After his run-in with Darcamius' scouts the other night, Seth restricted me to the cabin again, refusing me any outdoors time. He became overbearing and protective practically overnight. He used to let me spend some time in the woods as long as I didn't stay outside for too long, but now he was more controlling of my activities — refusing me any freedom. It had only been seven days of confinement, and already the walls were closing in on me. I couldn't take it anymore — I needed to get out.

He'd mentioned earlier in the morning that he would be leaving to get more supplies, which was my chance to pressure him from some fresh air. Perhaps he would let me go with him? I would be safe if he was by my side. No demon would be able to get his paws on me if I had Seth protecting me, right? So, where was the harm in me being his traveling companion?

After he collected his empty canvas bags and wallet from one of the drawers in the kitchen, Seth headed towards the door. I followed after him hastily.

"Where are you going?" I inquired keenly.

He turned his head around to glance at me. "I told you. We need more supplies. I'm going into town."

"Right ..." I responded slowly. Then, after giving him a bright smile I asked, "Can I come with you?"

Seth raised his left brow at me and smirked.

"What's so funny?"

"I could sense your desperation all morning, Lilianna," he said. "I knew it was only a matter of time before you asked to leave."

I frowned at him and replied, "And you think that's funny?"

"I think your behavior is immature, which I must admit is a little amusing."

"Immature? I'm not immature because I want to get out of this cabin, Seth. I'm going crazy being stuck in here day in and day out."

Seth sighed and responded, "It's only been a week."

"Exactly, and already I can't stand it," I told him loudly.

He shook his head at me and turned back around. "I'm sorry you feel that way, Lily, but it's not safe for you to wander around the woods. Not after what happened the other night."

"Then let me go with you! You'll protect me."

"It's not a good idea. I may be able to protect you, but I don't want to put you in any more danger. Why can't you understand that?"

"The only thing I understand is that you want to keep me locked up in this cabin like a prisoner!"

Seth's grey eyes sparked at my comment. "You know that's not true, Lily."

"Isn't it?"

"Of course not!"

"Then please let me step outside! Just for a minute," I whined, crossing my arms with impatience. "I'm dying in here!"

Seth, standing firmly between me and the door, placed his hands on his hips and replied, "No, Lilianna. I'm sorry, but it's not safe."

I exhaled loudly, shaking my head as I glared back at him. "This isn't fair, Seth! You said I was safe as long as I stayed within the barrier—"

"I know what I said, Lily," he interrupted me strongly. "But things have changed! Darcamius' scouts searching this area was not a coincidence. More will come … and we have to be on the defensive."

"I understand the danger—"

Seth frowned at me and spat, "No! You obviously don't, Lilianna! You have no idea what my father's demons will do to you if they find you. They'll take you by force — they will do whatever is necessary so long as they bring you back to my father alive. You can't even begin to imagine the horrors those monsters can inflict upon you."

"I know, Seth. I just need to get out of this gloomy cabin for a little while. I promise I'll be careful!"

He sighed. "I'm sorry. I can't slip up again and give my father the upper hand. I won't do it."

"But, Seth—"

"No buts, Lilianna. That's my say on the matter and it's final. Don't ask me to leave again."

"You can't do this to me! I'll suffocate if I stay locked up in this stupid cabin!"

"I apologize," he said with a bow of this head. "But it's for the best."

That was all he had to say on the matter, and he had made himself painfully clear. Without another word, he walked out of the cabin, both bags slung over his left shoulder. I glared at the back of his black head, resisting the urge to toss a book at it. How could he take my freedom away from me? It was cruel and unjust. He had no right to treat me like a hostage!

He said it was for the best, but best for whom? Not me. Why did it even matter if more scouts were lurking nearby? Seth would just dispose of them the same way he had the others. What was the big deal then? He wasn't even afraid of them; he had practically laughed about his cuts and bruises, which had magically healed overnight. No, I knew the true reason he wanted me to stay put. Seth was like any man I'd ever known — all he wanted was to control me. *Well, if he thinks I'm going to put up with his chauvinism, he had another thing coming!*

I trudged over to the couch and sat down with a loud cry of exasperation. As I sat there, curling my hands into fists of rage, a brilliant idea popped into my head. He was gone now — for almost an entire day. The nearest town was approximately two hundred miles away, and he wouldn't be back here for hours. When Seth told me we were isolated, he meant it. While he was gone I could sneak out, do some exploring, and be back before he returned. It was the perfect plan.

The only factor I was worried about was leaving the safety of the barrier. No matter how furious I was, I didn't want Darcamius creeping up on me in the middle of the woods without Seth's protection. But

222

perhaps the demons wouldn't be able to sense me if I was only out for a few hours or so. I wouldn't even remain outside of the barrier too long.

And then it was settled. I was leaving — just for a short while to clear my head. I needed the escape, and nothing but fresh air would soothe my itch. On the walk to my bedroom, I wondered where I was to go. I didn't want to remain just beyond the cabin, I wanted to see something new. If I was going to risk Seth's trust, I wanted it to count. There had to be something worth visiting in these woods.

The Swift River popped into my head, but I figured it was too far away — and I wouldn't know where to begin looking. When the hot springs sprang to mind, my pulse quickened with excitement. It was the perfect spot to go for a little R&R, which was exactly what I needed. I pulled an extra change of clothes out of my drawers and grabbed a towel from the bathroom, stuffing everything inside Seth's red backpack.

I gave the interior around me one last look before I hurried out of the front door. The minor guilt I'd been feeling only seconds before melted away when the sun's warm beams caressed my skin, and I smiled with joy. No longer confined to Seth's dismal cabin, I felt a rush of excitement flow through me. With a smile I hurried down the trail, eager for the small adventure I was about to partake in.

Hot springs here I come!

Chapter Fourteen

I'd been walking for nearly fifteen minutes when I began to despair. I knew I had to find the spring fast — before Seth got wind of my disappearance. He would most certainly try his hardest to find me before the sun fell, and there was a nagging thought in the back of my mind that maybe this wasn't such a good idea after all. I did not want to endure a half-demon's wrath.

I ignored those doubtful feelings though and continued through the woods, not exactly sure where I was going, but remaining optimistic. The hot springs couldn't be too far away; we'd passed them on our journey to Seth's cabin. As I traveled, I tied red ribbons I'd found in one of the kitchen drawers around various branches and bushes to mark my trail, in case I did get lost. At least I could make it back to the cabin no matter if I found the springs or not. I was smart enough to have a backup plan.

It was strangely silent in the woods as I trekked further from the cabin, save for the chirps of birds and the sound of the wind blowing the branches above my head. As I walked alone, I kept a lookout for anything menacing or life-endangering nearby. The coast was clear, but Seth's lectures about the barrier echoed in my head, clouding my judgment. I disregarded them. I would be fine. I wouldn't be gone for too long anyway. Just a dip in the springs and I would hurry home soon after. I had nothing to fear.

Twenty minutes turned to an hour, and before I knew it I was out of ribbons. I sighed, disappointed that I had failed. What a waste of my time. Maybe Seth had been right all along. There really was no use in wandering these woods. It was just one big labyrinth of trees. But when I completely gave up all hope and turned to walk the long journey back to the cabin, I heard the sound of water splashing.

My face lit up and I paused, trying to discern where the sound was coming from. I began to follow the sound, pushing back branches and bushes. I was off of the trail now, but I picked up my pace, hurrying in the direction of what I knew undoubtedly would be the hot springs.

When the glorious spring came into view I squealed with delight, running towards it at full speed. The water sparkled in the sunlight, and I could feel the heat radiating from its surface. I'd never had the pleasure of swimming in a genuine hot springs before, so I was pretty stoked. Before I had time to catch my breath I was stripping off my clothes and jumping into the springs buck naked.

The warm water soothed my soul, and I found myself gleaming with glee. After wading deeper into the spring, I gazed curiously over the environmental Jacuzzi. Large boulders made a sort of barrier in the springs, and there were a few jagged rocks sitting high out of the water and towering above my head. I swam away from them in silly fear they would topple over on my head. That would be just my luck.

My muscles loosened while I soaked, my stress fading away. The relaxation was much needed, and I found that my guilt over escaping the confinement of the cabin erased from my mind. There was nothing to fear — I was fine. As I lay floating on the water's surface, I wondered why Seth was so paranoid. Nothing had harmed me yet, and I'd been outside of the barrier long past an hour.

As I continued to float around, I contemplated what my parents assumed had become of me. No doubt they thought I was dead — or worse. Had they given up hope on my return? I would've given anything to let them know I was okay, but I knew it wasn't possible. Seth shot down the idea last week when I asked him if he could telephone them for me. He had explained it would be unwise to get my parents involved in the matter, and I agreed with him. I didn't want them to be in any danger.

The day passed by slowly with only the hot spring and my thoughts to keep me occupied, and when I began to grow bored and wrinkled, I decided it was time to head back. I swam to the edge near the rocks, and as I was about to hoist myself out of the water, I heard the loud boom of thunder. I gasped, noticing that the once blue and cloudless sky had grown considerably darker in the last few minutes. Fear settled in the pit of my stomach and I hurried out of the water, running towards my backpack. I pulled out a fresh change of clothes and quickly put them on. When I went to slide my feet into my tennis shoes, a loud cry startled me stiff.

My gaze darted to the sky, and I gasped as I watched two large winged creatures fall from above. They were massive, and when they swooped down towards the springs, I didn't have to guess that they were demons. They landed simultaneously with ease, both crouched, their heads bowed to the ground. When the demons finally rose, I got a closer look at their grisly appearances.

Four red eyes studied me, sunk into pale grey faces, which were oblong and very goblin-like. Both were clothed in black sheathes and wearing large black boots. There was nothing human about these two, and that gruesome fact almost brought me to tears. I backed away from them slowly, disgusted when they began to sneer at me with intense satisfaction.

I felt sick to my stomach, contemplating my options. No matter how strong or terrifying the demons were, I couldn't just stand there and wait for them to take me away. I had to act fast — think of some way to ditch them. But when they advanced towards me, I knew that wasn't going to be an easy feat.

"Stay back!" I ordered them, holding up my hands. "Don't come any nearer!"

The demons laughed at me and increased their pace. One of them stretched out his fingers, the nails on his hand extending at least ten inches long. He pointed them menacingly in my direction and said, "Come here, girl."

I screamed and turned to run, but I never stood a chance. Said demon grabbed me by my shoulders and pushed me to the ground. I cried out — mostly from shock — and tried to crawl away from him. He was too quick for me though. In a flash, he wrapped his hand around my calf, squeezing the muscle cruelly.

"You're not going anywhere, precious," he said with a growl, digging his nails into my flesh.

I winced from the harsh pain, and began to squirm, hoping to wiggle my way out of his grasp. This only angered the demon more, and before I had a chance to brace myself, he dug his nails deeper. I gasped, tears rolling down my cheeks ... but I couldn't give up. No matter how much it hurt, I preferred to die fighting than to succumb to his demands.

"Let go of me!" I yelled, sinking my fingers into the soft soil.

The demon laughed cruelly at my desperation, and I felt his nails in my legs vibrate with each chuckle. "All right. Enough fun. Let's get the human back to Darcamius," he said to his accomplice.

The other demon nodded, his red eyes sparking with excitement. "He's going to be very pleased with us when we show up with her."

"Yes, I believe he will be," he said, retracting his nails from my tender skin. With a grunt he tossed me up and over his shoulder, squeezing me when I began to kick my legs. "Knock it off!" he growled angrily.

"Please ..." I begged. "Let me go."

The demon simply laughed and squeezed my body tighter, causing me to gasp from the discomfort. I continued to cry when the demon began to walk, and as terrified as I was of him, I knew I had to do something soon. After everything I and the others had gone through, I couldn't let Darcamius win.

I didn't have to do anything though. Seth dropped out of the sky as fast as a lightning bolt, and my mouth dropped in astonishment when I saw them — the vast black wings protruding from his back.

"Seth?" I whispered with amazement when he flapped his wings. The demon holding me hostage grunted at the sight of my savior.

"Get lost, Septhim ... before you get yourself hurt. We have no business with you. All we want is the human."

"Let her go, Jargeen!" Seth replied angrily, his beautiful grey eyes now black, emotionless orbs.

I gasped at his new appearance. After all the time we'd spent together, as Seth glared down Jargeen he finally looked like his true self — like a half-demon.

Jargeen's accomplice laughed, his red eyes narrowing at Seth. "Jargeen may have no quarrel with you, Septhim, but I on the other hand would love to see you bleed to death all over this godforsaken forest."

Seth grinned and pushed back his long

black hair. "Caroothe, I'm surprised to see you so supercilious. After our last fight against each other, do you honestly want to risk your life again?"

The demon Caroothe growled, his face twisting with fury. "How dare you, halfling! You have no right to speak to me that way!"

With another confident smile, Seth added, "Just let Lilianna go and I will spare your pathetic life."

Caroothe sneered at Seth and stepped directly in front of Jargeen and me, making his stand. "If you want her, you'll have to get through me first, Septhim. And this time, I'm going to make sure I kill you — I'm going to rip you apart!"

Seth laughed and shook his head. "Have it your way."

With a glare, Seth raised his wings, and as fast as he had come down, he shot back up into the sky, twirling high among the dark clouds. I watched him fly with a restless heart, praying for his safety. Was he really going to fight these horrid demons? I didn't know how tough Seth was when compared to other demons, but if he wasn't strong, well, at least he knew how to talk a big game.

Caroothe took to the sky too, his wings smaller and less noticeable than Seth's. I studied the demon's wings as he flew away; the bones protruding out of the tip of his wings scared me. Caroothe didn't have feathers on his wings like Seth had; his looked more like a bat's, and it was kind of surreal to be comparing demon wings. I still couldn't believe that these ... things ... actually existed. They were like something out of a nightmare.

I heard a cry from above and my eyes darted along the treetops anxiously, afraid to learn the source of the sound, but my heart warmed with relief when I saw Seth was actually winning the fight. One of

Caroothe's wings was battered pretty badly, and it seemed he could hardly keep himself in the air. Then, in the blink of an eye, Seth soared into Caroothe at a force so powerful the demon was smacked clear across the forest. I searched the sky for Caroothe, afraid he would reappear to finish the fight. But after a few seconds passed, he never showed.

"Pathetic," Jargeen grunted, gripping me tighter. "I knew he wasn't going to stand a chance."

"Ow!" I hollered from his painful grip. "You're hurting me!"

"Good."

I watched with nervous eyes as wings began to protrude from Jargeen's back, wings similar to Caroothe's, and I almost had a heart attack when I realized that he was trying to escape with me unnoticed.

"Seth, help!" I screamed, as Jargeen jumped into the air.

Thankfully, Seth caught the demon just in time. He flew in front of us, spreading out his large wings, preventing Jargeen from passing by. "Put her down, Jargeen!" His black eyes sparked with anger.

Jargeen sneered at Seth's request. "Why are these humans so important to you, Septhim? I can understand your father's ruse to populate the human world with halflings, but you ... I don't understand why you care so much if this girl lives or dies."

"That's none of your concern, Jargeen," Seth replied sharply. "Just let her go. Now."

"Suppose I don't, Septhim? What are you going to do about it?"

"I think you know the answer to that question, Jargeen."

With a short laugh, Jargeen shook his head and said, "Your concern for this girl is useless. Don't you understand, Septhim? Humans have no remorse for our kind. They fear us — all of us, including half-demons. This girl will never accept you or your help. She can't be trusted."

"But I can trust you, Jargeen?" Seth asked with a huff. "Don't you dare speak to me about loyalty to my demonic ties. You and the rest of the purebloods would rather die than accept me as your own. I'm not as naïve as you think. I know what I am. I'm a half-demon; I belong nowhere — with no one."

"I see. Well, if you're not with us, then you're against us, and I can't let you interfere with Darcamius' plans. He gave strict orders to dispose of anyone who gets in our way."

Seth smirked at Jargeen's threat and replied, "I guess you're going to have to kill me then, because I will never let my father touch a hair on Lilianna's head!"

"You are a fool, Septhim Ananias. But so be it."

Jargeen removed me from his shoulder and dropped me to the ground. I grimaced when my shoulder collided with the hard earth. Jargeen had only been hovering a few feet in the air, but the fall was still large enough to pack a punch. I quickly forgot my pain though as I watched Jargeen fly at Seth, his black claws outstretched.

With a fierce howl, Jargeen went to strike at Seth's shoulder, but he evaded and retaliated with a swift kick in the stomach, which propelled Jargeen into a large tree trunk. This seemed to infuriate Jargeen, and in a flash he was back to attacking Seth, trying to damage his wings. He swiped his claws at the feathers, and I watched in horror when clumps of feathers fell from the sky.

"Seth, watch out!" My heart was racing with fear as I watched the two demons fight

240

each other above my head. If Seth lost, I was doomed. He couldn't let Jargeen get the best of him. He had to beat him — he just had to! If he didn't, Darcamius would …

I stopped my foolish thoughts there, as shame washed over me. I felt horribly selfish for only caring about my own wellbeing. There Seth was, battling a very scary looking demon on account of me, and I could only worry about me. It was my fault and my fault alone that I was in this current predicament. If only I had obeyed Seth's orders, none of this would have happened, and Seth wouldn't be risking his life to rescue me.

Then the battle took a turn for the better. After stunning him with his wings, Seth grabbed hold of the demon by the neck and swung him high above his head. He held Jargeen's body upright for a split second before flinging him straight down to the ground, with a force so powerful his

body made a crater in the forest floor. I
gasped and eyed the crater warily. Was the
fight really over? Was the demon dead?

Seth descended from the sky, landing
smoothly next to the crater, and I watched
in awe as his wings retracted into his back.
As he stood on the edge of the hole, his
black eyes studied Jargeen's motionless
body intently. I wandered closer to get a
better look, but Seth held up his hand and
ordered me to stay back. Then, Jargeen's
head popped up out of the crater, but
before I even had a chance to scream, Seth
struck his head hard, knocking it clean off. I
gagged and looked away, the sight
repulsing me. As I struggled to regain my
bearings, I felt a pair of hands pushing me
back, away from the unpleasant scene.

"Don't look, Lily," Seth instructed me
sternly. "It'll only upset you further."

"You killed him," I whispered, still in
shock from the sight of Jargeen's blood.

Seth raised his brows at me and replied, "I didn't have a choice. It was either him or me. I chose me."

I nodded but said nothing. I knew why Seth had to kill Jargeen, but his means still didn't comfort me. I had witnessed his strength firsthand after all, and I was a little shaken by this abilities. Seth was powerful — way more than he had let on. He had taken care of those two demons without any trouble. If it was that easy to kill a demon, I wondered how easily he could dispose of a human. He would probably need his pinky finger and nothing more.

"Lilianna, are you injured?" Seth asked, his voice snapping me out of my thoughts.

I glanced down at my calf, where the demon had stabbed me with his nails, and frowned. "Not really. That demon Jargeen cut up my leg a little, but I'm okay."

"Let me look at your leg," Seth said, and he then dropped down to his knees to examine my calf. He traced his fingers over the wounds and sighed. "These are pretty deep. We'll have to treat them as soon as we get back to the cabin."

"I'm okay, really," I told him calmly. "It doesn't even hurt."

Seth's grey eyes flashed with worry as he said, "It may not hurt now, but a scratch from a demon can cause a human great sickness if left untreated."

I bit my lip, afraid to ask what might happen to me if he couldn't mend the wound.

"The sickness is always different," he continued. "But it will consume you. Not many humans can survive after contracting it." Seth's voice cracked suddenly and his eyes quickly darted towards the ground. I froze, unsure of what to say. His skin turned pale, and he seemed so helpless at that moment.

"Seth, are you all right? You look ...

frightened."

I found it hard to get those words out. It shocked me that Seth could look such a way — especially when it was on account of me.

"I'm upset, Lily. That's all," he remarked angrily, still staring at the ground while he tried his hardest to keep his temper in check. "If I had shown up only a minute later, you'd be—" He scowled then, and his hands clenched into a fist. The corners of his mouth twitched with rage as he asked, "What were you thinking?"

"Seth, I—" I tried to explain that I was sorry, but he wouldn't have it.

"You deliberately disobeyed me, Lilianna!" he interrupted loudly. "I have explained to you the dangers of the leaving the cabin — of leaving the barrier. You know the barrier can only protect you if you're within twenty feet of the cabin!"

"I know," I replied shortly. "I just—"

Seth's grey eyes narrowed at me as he added, "You just have a blatant disregard for your safety!"

His comment angered me. That wasn't the case. Of course I cared about my wellbeing; I just couldn't stand being cooped up inside that crusty old cabin any longer. I needed some fresh air — a change of scenery. But he wouldn't give me my freedom. Couldn't he understand that I wasn't like him? I couldn't hide from the world the way he did.

"That's not true, Seth!" I shot back. "I was careful!"

He smirked at my excuse. "Oh really? Careful, huh? Well, you were so careful, Lilianna, that you gave away your location to two of Darcamius' minions. And you're lucky it was only those two meager drones that showed up here. What if Darcamius had come to collect you himself? What would you have done then, Lily?"

"I don't know!" I yelled, my hands balled tightly at my sides.

Seth was driving me over the edge. I wasn't a child. I knew that what I did was wrong ... but I just couldn't shake that empty feeling I'd been carrying around for weeks. Day after day we held up in that cabin, with only books and chores to keep us occupied. I couldn't live that way — and he couldn't expect me to. I needed adventure ... an escape, even if it was a childish idea.

My anger at him withered away when I detected the disappointed glint in his eye. It was at that moment that I realized Seth was only upset with me because he cared. If he didn't care, he wouldn't have dropped out of the sky in the nick of time to defend me like he had. I had disobeyed him, yes, but he still put up with me. Why was that?

"I'm sorry, Seth," I told him suddenly, carefully meeting his guarded eyes. "I shouldn't have run off like that. It was wrong of me."

Seth seemed to accept my apology, because his tense expression eased away. With a deep sigh, he replied, "It's all right, Lilianna. I know this hasn't been easy on you, and I can understand your need to slip away, but you should have told me you wanted to go to the springs. I would've taken you myself had you only asked."

"What? But you said that you didn't want me leaving the barrier! You said it wouldn't be safe for me to travel through the woods!"

"It wouldn't be wise, no, but I don't want your misery on my hands. I should have given you more space — allowed you to escape the cabin, if only for a few hours." Seth pointed to the wound on my leg and added, "Perhaps if I had, this would not have happened to you. I apologize."

Now he was accepting the blame for

my reckless actions? I couldn't let him do that; it was my fault and my fault alone. I shook my head and said, "Don't apologize to me, Seth. I was the one who ran off. I deserve the blame for almost getting taken."

"It doesn't matter who's at fault," he replied softly. "All that matters now is that you're safe."

I smiled, grateful to him for showing up when he had. He was my hero, as usual.

"Thanks for rescuing me. Again. I thought I was doomed for sure."

Seth returned the smile and replied, "It's all right, Lilianna. You don't have to thank me. As long as I'm around, no harm will come to you. I promise you that." He gestured towards the trees and asked, "Ready to go back?"

I nodded, and after picking up the backpack off of the ground, I joined Seth's side. As we walked back towards the trail, I stole one last look at the hole in the earth —

at the beheaded demon that now lay dead
inside it.

Chapter Fifteen

"So, what's with the wings?"

We had just sat down to dinner, and I figured there was nothing more interesting a topic for discussion. My mind was still reeling over yesterday's chaotic events. I couldn't help it. I had almost got taken — and I would've been too, had it not been for Seth and his amazing abilities.

Seth raised his head from his plate to glance at me. "What about my wings?"

I shrugged and took a swig of juice. "I was just wondering about them, that's all. Do all demons have wings? Jargeen has them — er, had."

Seth shook his head and replied, "No, Lily, not all demons have wings."

"How do the others get around then? Do they have super speed like you?"

With a slight smile, Seth said, "I

suppose most demons have a heightened speed, yes, but the older and more powerful demons can ... well, sort of teleport, if you will."

I stared blankly at him, the word teleport stunning me into a stupor. "Really?"

Seth nodded. "Yes. Demons have a wide range of unique abilities and attributes — many which would shock the human race."

"Like?" I pressed eagerly.

"Like teleporting, for instance, and being able to create force fields and barriers. Some demons can also turn invisible, breathe underwater, or create fireballs or waves of electricity. And a few demons, like me, have wings and can fly."

"Cool," I muttered, stabbing my fork at a piece of broccoli on my plate. I brought it to my mouth, and after chewing it slowly, let it slide down my throat. It was so delicious — the best broccoli I'd ever had in my life. Seth was an amazing cook; he could even make broccoli taste amazing. I studied him while he ate, wondering what other amazing talents he had up his sleeves — the human ones anyway.

When he realized I was watching him, Seth stared back at me. "What is it, Lily?"

"Nothing," I replied quickly, going for another piece of broccoli. I smiled when I took a bite, relishing the burst of flavor in my mouth. I felt sort of useless. Here I was, a young woman who couldn't cook to save her life. What did I bring to this team? Nothing. Seth did the fighting, the defending, the storytelling, and even the cooking. All I ever did was the screaming and cowering.

Seth raised his brow knowingly at me and said, "Lily, you don't have to beat yourself up about not being able to cook. It's not a big deal. I don't mind it one bit."

I frowned at him and rolled my eyes.

"There you go again. Reading my thoughts! Have you ever entertained the idea that maybe people don't want their thoughts read? That some things are private, and you shouldn't just pop into a person's thoughts whenever you feel like it?"

His expression turned grave after my outburst, and he bowed his head in shame. "You're right, Lilianna. I apologize. I'll stop from this moment on."

"Thank you very much. I appreciate it," I replied happily, popping a chunk of tomato in my mouth. After chewing it, I asked, "What else are you good at, Seth? If you don't mind me asking."

"Do you mean human-wise?"

"Yes."

Seth scratched his head as he thought, and I found the action sort of funny. "Well, I'm good at hunting and fishing," he finally said, looking rather pleased with himself.

I smirked at his response, "That's it?"

254

"Hmm," he replied softly, still thinking. "I can ride a horse fairly well."

I laughed. "Wow. So you can cook, hunt, and ride horses. All of which are fairly primitive."

Seth smiled and laughed as he replied, "I suppose they are, yes."

A question popped into my head, and before I had a chance to think it over, I asked, "Can you dance?"

"Dance? No, I can't say that I know how."

"Really?"

"I haven't had many opportunities to dance, Lily," Seth told me with a roll of his eyes. "Half-demon remember?" Then his mood changed suddenly and he frowned, looking off, his expression turning grave. "I was asked to dance once, but I never got the chance."

I bit my lip, the urge to dance filling my entire body. Finally, something I had the upper hand on. With a smile I stood from the table and walked over to him. I motioned for him to stand, but he simply stared blankly at me.

"Get up," I told him eagerly.

"What for?"

"I'm going to teach you how to dance."

Seth's grey eyes flashed and he seemed hesitant. "I don't think that's such a good idea, Lily."

I shook my head and replied, "I'm not going to take no for an answer, Seth Ananias. Now stand up and join me in the middle of the living room." I wandered over towards the vacant space near the couch without him, where I waited with my arms crossed.

When he realized I wasn't going to budge from my spot, he stood from the table and joined me.

"Thank you," I told him with a smile. I glanced around the room, looking for some sort of CD player or stereo. When I found no such device, I asked, "Is there anything in this cabin that plays music?"

Seth frowned and replied, "I don't think so—" He paused and glanced behind him, at the large cabinet sitting near the open hallway. "Actually, I believe there is such a thing. Mathias used it often."

"Mathias?"

"The man who used to live here — the one that carved the flower into the door."

"Oh," I replied softly.

I watched Seth wander over towards the cabinet, and he opened it slowly to reveal an old record player. He picked it up and wandered back over, setting it down gently on the coffee table near the couch. After blowing away the layer of dust that coated it, Seth cranked the lever and lifted the needle onto the record that was already placed inside. An old, fast tune drifted from the player.

I smiled at the sound of the old music, and beckoned Seth to join my side once more. "Here, take my hand," I instructed firmly, raising my right hand into the air. Seth reached for my hand, but met my eyes hesitantly. Without warning, I took a slow step backwards, motioning him to follow my lead. A few shaky steps afterwards I proceeded to teach him the waltz.

The only reason I even knew how to dance was because of my mother. The summer I turned fourteen, she decided I needed structure — probably because I'd been caught shoplifting with my friend Tara a month earlier — and enrolled me in a ballroom dance class. I hated being trapped in that old dance studio while the rest of my friends were on the beach or at parties, but even though I wasn't very fond of learning ballroom, it stuck and I paid enough attention during that long summer to be able to teach it to Seth.

His stance was a tad rigid at first, but after a while he began to loosen up and really enjoy himself. I smiled at the sight of his happiness as we twirled along the small living area in the cabin, and I too couldn't conceal my excitement. Seth was the first person I had danced the waltz with that wasn't over forty-five. Technically, he was the oldest person I had ever danced with, but he sure didn't look it.

Without my instruction, Seth surprised me by spinning me around gently. He caught me with ease, his eyes twinkling with delight. "I like this," he said softly, gazing keenly at me.

"Me too," I replied faintly, the look in his eyes startling my soul.

Then the song abruptly switched over to a soft ballad and we stopped dancing. I eyed Seth cautiously, wondering what I should do. It was a sort of awkward moment for me as I stared up at him, still feeling breathless from his intense gaze. Seth didn't notice the change in my mood though.

"How do you dance to this type of music?" he asked me innocently. "The same way?"

I ignored all of the confusing emotions I was feeling at that moment and tried to focus on entertaining him. I didn't want to scare him off by acting odd. Besides, what did I have to feel awkward about? We were just a couple of friends dancing to kill time. There was nothing going on between us ... right? If that was the case, why did I feel like I was on cloud nine?

"Like this," I said, with a slight smile, and wrapped my arms around his waist. I waited a moment for him to copy me, and then, without thinking, I laid my head against his chest. We said nothing as we swayed gently to the soft music, remaining in the same spot for the most part.

Seth was so close to me I could taste him; his smell was intoxicating, and I couldn't stop myself from falling into a silent bliss. When my eyes slipped shut, all I concentrated on was the faint sound of his heartbeat. I felt so safe at that moment — as if I was in another place or time. My heart was fluttering, and before I could stop myself, my lips let out a soft sigh.

"Lilianna?"

I lifted my head cautiously to gaze at him, my cheeks the reddest they had ever been. "Sorry, don't mind me, Seth. It's just been a long time since I've danced ... this way with someone."

He nodded at me and seemed to understand, but I noticed that he was holding back; his beautiful grey eyes gave him away.

"What's wrong, Seth? Have I made you uncomfortable?" I asked, feeling utterly embarrassed. "I apologize—"

"No," he interrupted me quickly. "Don't apologize, Lily. I'm alright."

"Okay, if you're sure...."

We continued to slow dance, both of us simply staring at the other. The serious look on Seth's face began to make me a little uncomfortable, and after awhile I began to laugh, the awkward silence, and the stern expression on my dance partner's face finally getting to me.

"What's so funny?" Seth asked.

"You are," I told him with a laugh. "So serious all of the time."

He frowned. "You find my temperament funny?"

I pouted at the gloomy sound of his question. "Don't be upset, Seth. I just think you should have fun every once and while. You know ... let yourself go."

"Easy for you to say. You weren't born a monster."

"You're not a monster, Seth," I told

262

him sternly. "Don't call yourself that."

He glared down at me, my response offending him. "How can you say that? You've seen what I can do! What I truly am!"

"Don't sell yourself short! You're an amazing person!"

Seth snorted. "Who has demon wings."

I frowned and shook my head at his negativity. "It's not your fault you're half-demon. You have no control over the matter, but it doesn't make you who you are, Seth."

"Lily—"

"No, listen to me! It's what you do with your strength and abilities that defines you. You've risked everything to protect me and the other women from Darcamius. So no, you're not a monster, Seth. You're a hero."

Seth glanced down at me, and the anger on his face melted away. After a moment, he finally smiled and said, "Thank you, Lilianna, for your kind words."

"I don't want your thanks, Seth. I want you to open up those grey eyes of yours and see how amazing you truly are."

He chuckled. "I don't know if I ever will, but for you, Lily, I will try."

"Good."

We resumed dancing until the song finished, and when we finally broke apart, I knew that whatever previous anger or resentment I'd felt towards him had vanished. It was like magic.

"Lily, I want to thank you for teaching me how to dance. I enjoyed it very much."

"You're welcome," I replied, smiling.

Seth smiled back, his grey eyes wavering as he looked me over. He seemed as if he wanted to say more, but whatever it was, he was having a hard time getting it past his lips. Finally his hesitation fell away and he said, "I was thinking about what happened the other day at the spring. If I hadn't been so stubborn and kept you locked up in this cabin, your encounter with Darcamius' minions wouldn't have happened."

"Seth—"

He held up his hand to silence me. "Please, let me finish. We have a long stay here, and I want you to be happy. If that means I have to chaperone you on hikes through the woods or accompany you to the spring, then so be it."

"What are you saying?" I asked him eagerly, excitement swelling up inside my chest.

Seth grinned, obviously pleased by my thrilled tone. "I'm saying that tomorrow, we can go wherever you choose. We can visit the hot springs again if you like, or take a hike. We can even go visit the Swift River—"

"Yes! There!" I interrupted. "I want to go to the river."

"All right then, it's settled," he smiled.

"We'll head for the Swift River first thing in the morning."

I beamed up at him, surprised by the sudden change in his nature. I knew him well enough to know he was all about safety first and fun last. Whatever the reason, though, I didn't care. I was just glad we could finally leave the confines of the cabin. I was so happy, and before I could control my rush of emotions, I threw my arms around him, hugging him tightly.

"Thank you, Seth. You have no idea how happy this makes me."

"I'm glad. Your happiness is all that matters to me," Seth replied kindly, and returned the hug. We remained in an embrace for some time before Seth broke away. His eyes glimmered as they stared me down, and I couldn't help but notice the adoration hiding within them.

Then, after giving me a keen grin, Seth said, "We should get a good night's rest for the journey ahead us. We have a lot of walking to do tomorrow."

"Okay," I nodded, knowing he was probably right. He usually was.

I walked over towards the hallway, but I stopped in the threshold to glance back at him, surprised by the pleased expression on his face.

Sending him a warm smile, I said, "Thanks again for doing this for me, Seth."

"Whatever you wish for, Lily — as long as it's reasonable, I will deliver it to you."

I smiled at him once more, knowing he was true to his word. "Goodnight," I told him softly.

"Goodnight," he replied, and I wandered down the hall towards my room, a questionable feeling of delight tickling the insides of my stomach. I didn't know which made me happiest, the fact that Seth was taking me to the Swift River or that he had looked at me the way he had tonight. Either way, I was ecstatic to be able to go on an actual outing ... but more so that this time Seth would be by my side the entire day.

Chapter Sixteen

It was a bleak and foggy night, perfect for the eerie events that were about to unfold. As I hurried down the dark streets of town, the grey brick and stones of the buildings glimmered in the moonlight, my only illumination; most of the torches and lantern's were extinguished at this hour. There weren't many persons out and about, save for a few prostitutes standing idly in the alleyways, and the town drunk lying on his back in the gutter. I was alone; there was no one to share my burden with.

The stillness of the night only worried me further, and my heart trembled with anticipation as I hurried towards the convent — the one place I had called my home. The mysterious man had said it would soon be destroyed at the hand of a demon. But I could not let that happen — all of my sisters would surely perish with it. It was my responsibility to save them. After all, the demon sought me and me alone. There would be no bloodshed on my behalf tonight.

I had sneaked out of the convent, an act I'm ashamed to admit thrilled me. Although I had escaped its holy walls many times before, this time I had good reason. A strange man with grey eyes visited me in the church the other day, explaining he needed to desperately speak with me. He couldn't divulge his secret in front of the other sisters, but he asked to meet the following night at the local tavern in town. I would've dismissed him, but the forlorn look on his face gave his sincerity away. The man knew I was unsure to trust him, but he swore he was a gentleman. I had nothing to go by but his word, and for some reason I believed him.

When I met up with him earlier this

evening, he explained I shouldn't fear him — that he didn't intend to hurt me. He was so mysterious about his identity when I asked, as if he was ashamed to tell me; he later confessed it was of no importance who he was. I begged him to divulge the meaning of this gathering, the curious looks from the patrons in the bar causing me worry. The man said he knew of an attack on the convent tonight — and the attack, he said, was being led by a demon. He then proceeded to tell me a story of a young woman being brutally raped and killed by the same demon, and how I was her reincarnation. The stranger said that the demon was after me, and that he would stop at nothing to kidnap me. His intention? To procreate with me.

I would not have believed his bizarre tale, but I recalled a nightmare I'd had only days before, of a young woman picking crops who met her death at the hands of a monster that only the devil himself could have created. The nightmare had felt strangely real, as if it were a memory. Realization hit me then, and I knew that this stranger was telling me the truth. If what he said was true, then that left me no time; I had to warn the other sisters before it was too late. I hurried out of the tavern, ignoring the man's pleas of caution. There was nothing he could do to stop me; it was my duty to protect my congregation.

When the age-old building came into view, I smiled, grateful that the demon had not reached it before I had. There was still a chance I could save everyone. I rushed onto the grounds, ignoring the caretaker's curious glances as he passed me on his nightly round. He had a right to be interested in my whereabouts. It was not acceptable for a young woman, especially a woman of God, to be walking around the streets of Shalldt at night. The penalty for such conduct would be severe, and had it been any other night I would've begged for his silence. However, with the pressing dark matter at hand, I prayed he woke the priests. It would save me the trouble.

Without a moment's hesitation, I entered our quarters and was surprised to find Sister Margaret awake, sitting upright in bed with a book in her lap. She glared at me from behind her thin spectacles, a pious rant near to spilling past her lips. Before she had a chance to scold me, I ran at her, preaching the strange man's warning. Her blue eyes widened from shock, but when she peered closer at my grief-stricken face, she knew I was speaking the truth.

The next few minutes passed by in a blur. Sister Margaret took hold of the situation, as she usually did when a problem was introduced to her. She woke the other sisters in a hurry, ushering them out of the small housing without so much as a reason why. The sisters, clad in their thin white nightgowns, were bewildered by the situation. Sister Margaret held her tongue when the youngest members of our set badgered her with questions. I would not answer them either, afraid the sisters would act out in fear. I wanted only to protect them, even if it was from themselves.

The sisters filed out into the night, Sister Margaret leading them in prayers as she escorted them. I stayed back, knowing how dangerous I was. He could come at any moment, and I could not be around them when he surfaced. Relief washed over me when I noticed the priests hurrying out of the convent, anger and confusion etched on their weathered faces. I smiled, even as they studied me with disapproving eyes. I knew they had heard of my escape from the caretaker.

Sister Margaret pulled Father Jacob aside and explained the situation. I could tell by her shrill tone and extensive hand gestures that she was just as frightened as I was, if not more. However, she held face in front of the other sisters. The fathers, now aware of the situation, led the congregation from the grounds, rushing out onto the darkened streets of Shalldt. I stayed back, watching with tearful eyes as my sisters and the priests escaped without me. I knew it was better this way; I would only cause them danger if I remained in their group.

Suddenly, lightning ignited the sky, followed by a loud roar of thunder. An unsettling feeling of despair settled in my stomach and I glanced nervously at the night sky, expecting the worst. Had the demon finally come for me? A loud scream from the streets startled me, and my eyes darted in its direction. I shrieked from fear when I noticed a fellow sister, Sister Anne, lying in the street; her face pale, her right hand draped carefully over her heart.

A tall man towered over her body, causing me great worry. He was massive, and when he lifted his head and stared at me, I gasped at the sight of his eyes, which were black and soulless. Time stopped at that moment, and as we stared at each other I saw a glimpse of my nightmare and I knew who he was. I backed away instinctively and the demon grinned at me, now realizing my identity. He stepped over Sister Anne's body carelessly, lifting his hands out in front of him, and with a flick of his wrist he set them both aflame. My jaw dropped in astonishment, and before I had a chance to react, the demon threw two fireballs at the convent's towers.

The fire spread in a matter of seconds, eating every inch of the building. I wept at the sight of the flames, and anger crept into my soul. This demon was not going to destroy everything I loved. I wouldn't stand for it! I had to lure him away from the convent — from the others — before he caused more damage. He desired me and me alone. I knew if I left the holy grounds I would fall prey to his charms, but it was the only chance I had to save everyone from certain death.

Strength surged through me and I rushed back into the burning convent, hurrying through the smoky corridors, weaving in and out of empty rooms. When I made it to the kitchen, I paused by the door, eyeing the large butcher knife lying on the counter near the stove. I hardly believed it would serve me much use against the demon, but I could use it as a last resort if nothing else. I grabbed it swiftly and wrapped a cloth around the blade before thrusting it inside the pocket of my dress. I then ran out the door, feeling more confident than I had all night.

I breathed in the fresh air deeply as I ran towards the gardens, eyeing the surrounding area cautiously. There was a gate on the other end of the gardens that led out to the streets of Shalldt, near the tavern and the old inn. Perhaps the demon would search for me inside the convent and I would have a chance to escape. The presumption was doubtful, but it gave me hope nonetheless.

When I neared the end of the convent's large gardens, I sighed with relief when the black iron gate came into view and the demon was nowhere to be seen. I wasted no time. In a matter of seconds I unlatched the gate and ran off, keeping my eyes and ears alert, and I was surprised to find all of Shalldt's residents out in the street, standing idly by as the convent was engulfed by flames. They exchanged glances as I ran past them, but I ignored their curiosity and hurried on.

I kept running, my abdomen burning and my lungs fighting for oxygen. After a while, I had to slow down, keeping my attention fixed on the road ahead of me. As soon as I neared the edge of town, I couldn't resist the urge to glance back at the place I'd called home my whole life. My eyes welled with tears at the sight of the smoke rising in the night air, where I knew the convent sat burning. I prayed at that moment, not for my own safety, but for the sisters, fathers, and the people of the town. I prayed God would spare them from the demon's wicked wrath. Only he could keep them safe.

I turned back around to continue on, but a large figure standing in the middle of the road prevented me from taking another step. I eyed the dark outline fearfully, knowing full well who it was. He had caught up with me at last. With a deep breath, I grabbed the butcher knife from within my dress, the cloth falling from the blade to the ground. I held the knife in front of me and closed my eyes, praying for God's forgiveness for what I was about to do. A tear slipped down my cheek, for I knew he would not save me ... but I had no choice.

The demon glared at me, shouting at me to put down the knife, but I told him he would not corrupt me. I would rather condemn myself to an eternity in Hell than allow him to use my body for his twisted gain. With one last breath, I apologized to my lord and savior, placed the blade against my throat, and slashed the skin. A moment passed and I felt nothing. It was only when I felt a pair of arms circling me that I realized I was lying on the cold pavement.

I glanced up at the person holding me, surprised to find it was the stranger from the tavern — the one who had warned me of the demon. Blood stained his face, and I wondered if he was hurt. It took me a few seconds before I realized it was my blood that was covering him. I gasped, feeling myself growing weaker. He begged me to hold on, but it was no use, I was dying. I gave the stranger a weak smile and thanked him for his concern before closing my eyes — then everything went quiet.

Chapter Seventeen

We left the cabin around eleven, and much to my annoyance, Seth kept insisting that he carry me on the way to the river. He was always so cautious, as if he assumed his father was going to swoop out of the sky and nab me. Of course, I wouldn't have been surprised if his father actually tried to do just that □ but I didn't care. I wanted to walk the trail like a human being. I was sick and tired of being carried or slung over his shoulder like a ragdoll. I had legs, I could walk, and so I objected firmly. Besides, Seth had promised me that today we could do whatever I wanted to do, and I was going to hold him to that promise right down to the very last detail.

For the duration of the hike, neither of us spoke one word. I wanted to talk about

Louisa, seeing I'd just dreamed of her death the night before. There were things I was still curious about ☐ but I didn't want to spoil the day by talking about it. Seth's mood would turn sour for sure, and I just wanted to relax and pretend my life was normal, if only for a little while. Was it really so hard to go a day without a discussion about demons or death? I just wanted us to spend a peaceful afternoon together for once. I was sure he knew that was what I was thinking, and it's why he remained quiet. Seth really was being a gentleman about it all, and I was surprised.

When Seth told me that the Swift River was a magnificent sight, I hadn't really considered how magnificent it would be. I figured he was just trying to overplay it for my sake, to give me something to look forward to ... but when the trees around us started to fall away, giving me a clear view of the vast river, I gasped in awe. It was beautiful, full of rich color and wildlife. I had never seen anything so charming in all my life, even living in New Hampshire as long as I had.

As I watched the currents surge over various rocks and boulders, I felt a pang of homesickness and longed for my mother. She would have loved to see this □ she was a bigger fan of nature than I was. Our first family trip had been to Yellowstone National Park, and as boring as it sounds, it was actually pretty great. One of her old friends from school worked there, so we got to tour the area without any other groups. We were treated like celebrities ... but that wasn't the best part. I remember the satisfied look on my mother's face when a geyser blew sky high. That was the highlight of the trip for me, my mother having a great time. It was a special memory, something I was never going to forget.

I hurried towards the riverbank

excitedly, and watched with a smile as a giant green frog hopped along the rocky ground near my feet, headed for a large boulder sitting on the shore. I crouched down and observed it, amazed by how big it was. How odd it was of me to be amazed by a simple amphibian. I usually screamed at the sight of frogs, but after being cooped up in a cabin for a week, I was beginning to appreciate the simpler things in life ... and it was all thanks to Mr. Septhim.

"Lily!" Seth called out to me loudly, and I turned around to face him.

"What?" I asked Seth curiously as I rose.

Seth pointed upwards and my gaze followed the direction, noticing that a large cliff hung above us. I frowned and bit my lip, knowing exactly why he was showing it to me. He wanted to go up there. What was with this guy and heights? I cracked a smile when a highly improbable assumption passed through my mind. Blushing with nervousness, I wondered if he just wanted a chance to hold me.

Glancing back at Seth warily, I replied, "Alright, fine." Then I flashed a grin suddenly and mocked, "Go ahead. Do your demon stuff."

Seth's eyes sparked at my comment, but he ignored my bad humor and joined me at the edge of the river. "Hold on to me tight," Seth instructed, as he swiftly lifted me up.

I placed my arms around his neck securely and held on for my life when he leapt into the air. My stomach flipped from the speed of his jump and I glanced down nervously at the scenery below us. Bad idea. After staring wide-eyed at the various trees and rocks far beneath our feet, I began to hyperventilate from the elevation. Ugh, I hated heights. I shut my eyes quickly and nuzzled my face into Seth's shoulder, hoping it would ease my fear. He landed on the cliff only a few seconds later, and placed me down gently. It took me a moment to regain my composure, and I ignored Seth as he shook his head at me.

"It's not my fault," I wheezed, staring down gratefully at the rocky ground beneath my feet. I was extremely relieved to be standing once again.

"Why are you so afraid of heights, Lilianna?"

I started to pull my hair into a ponytail, but I remembered I didn't have a band around my wrist so I let the hair fall back down. "Because ... I just am, okay?" I said, not wanting to reminisce.

"*Because* is not an excuse, Lily," he replied.

I rolled my eyes and sighed. He wasn't going to stop asking until I told him the reason why. I knew him too well.

Upon crossing my arms swiftly, I

decided to share. "When I was six years old, I fell out of a tree in my backyard and broke my right arm. I had been playing outside all by myself. My mother had been inside resting, so she didn't hear my screams when I fell. I remember trying to grab every single branch on the way down, but I couldn't stop myself from falling. I've been terrified of heights ever since."

"I see ..." Seth replied softly, and he walked towards the edge of the cliff. He stared out towards the river and added, "I'm sorry if I made you uncomfortable by bringing you up here, Lily. I just assumed you would enjoy the view."

I bit my lip, feeling sort of embarrassed. Here he was, trying his hardest to make this experience special for me and I was being so inconsiderate. I could try to fight my fears for just one day, couldn't I? My gaze fixed on his back, I took a deep breath to try and settle my nerves before joining him at the cliff's edge.

"Seth, I —" My mouth closed swiftly when I noticed how amazing the view of the river was. From where we were standing, you could see far across the forest and the outline of the White Mountains in the distance. The Swift River seemed to almost originate from the mountains, and it was such a vast, incredible creek. The flowing water was crystal clear, and seemed to sparkle from the sun. It was breathtaking, and I felt privileged to be able to see such a vision.

"It's beautiful!" I gushed. "I don't think I've ever seen anything so amazing in all my life."

Seth smiled, and I think it was the first time I'd ever seen him smile sincerely.

"I'm glad you're pleased," he told me.

I glanced up into his bright eyes and smiled in return. "It's all thanks to you, Seth. Thank you."

"There's no need to thank me, Lily. I know how important this day was to you. I wanted it to be special," Seth said, still smiling.

I blushed and looked off, avoiding his heavy gaze. Did he really mean that? *He just said it, didn't he?* I bit my lip and tried to ignore the fire that had crept up my neck. What was I getting all worked up for? Seth and I were friends after all. It wasn't unusual for him to want to do something nice for me ... right?

I thought about how we had danced the night before, our arms wrapped around each other tightly. The way he had looked at me and held me in his arms ... he had been a dream. Just thinking about it gave me goose bumps. It had been a long time since a guy had treated me so tenderly.

Seth looked me over suddenly, his expression turning dark. His smile faded away, and his eyes turned to stone. I frowned, taken aback by the abrupt change in his mood, and wondered what caused it.

"Come on," he told me briskly. "I'll take you back down," and he gestured to lift me up.

I frowned. *Oh no. Was he reading my thoughts again? And we were having such a lovely time too.* I walked towards him and waited to be raised into his arms. My face was red with embarrassment as I toyed with the idea of asking him what was wrong. Who was I kidding? Seth would never admit something was amiss.

With a steep jump, Seth leapt off of the cliff. We landed down by the river before I had a chance to brace myself. He lowered me down to the ground swiftly and strode away without a word, towards a large tree positioned only a few feet away from the riverbank. I watched him settle underneath its shade, and I couldn't help but feel a little anxious. Why was he acting put off all of a sudden? Was it something I did?

I decided not to push him, and eyed the river with eagerness. As the stream lapped over various rocks and boulders, basking them in its crystal waters, I felt the urge to be caressed the same way. Why should those rocks have all the fun? I glanced casually at Seth before lifting my shirt over my head. He frowned upon noticing I was wearing a bathing suit.

"Lilianna," he called out to me warily. "What are you doing?"

"Going swimming. What does it look like, Septhim?" I shot back with a smirk.

I quickly tugged my jean shorts down to my ankles and kicked them aside, next to my shirt, before running towards the river's edge. Hesitant to just rush in, I dipped a toe into the water first, and I shivered from its temperature.

"If you want to go swimming, Lily, I'll

take you to the hot springs," Seth called out to me. "It's too dangerous to swim in the Swift River."

"No, I want to swim here. It'll be fine," I told him sternly. "Stop worrying so much."

Seth glared at me, but with a quiet grumble, he gave up the battle. "All right, fine. Just stay near the bank and keep away from the middle of the river. The currents will be too strong for you to fight — the stream will force you down with it."

"Okay," I promised, with a roll of my eyes.

After taking a deep breath to brace myself for the cold, I ran into the river, screaming as the cold water rushed over my midsection. It was freezing, but I didn't mind. As I splashed my arms about, I got used to the chill and began to really enjoy the water. After dunking my head underwater to wet my hair and face, I swam a few feet away from the bank, eyeing the center of the river warily. I knew I couldn't get too close, or else I would regret it. Seth would have my butt for disobeying him too.

With a soft sigh, I laid my head back against the water, allowing my body to rise towards the surface. I stared up at the bright blue sky, enjoying the way my face was warmed while the rest of my body remained cold. I cloud-watched for a while, until I began to feel too relaxed.

My eyes slipped shut as a tranquil sensation took over my body. I didn't have a care in the world. No thoughts of demons or death, or even my life back in Jackson. The whole world was shut out, and all that mattered was the gentle calm of the river — and that was just fine with me.

Then, as fast as it came, my tranquility melted away and fear took hold. I was unable to resist the darkness that began to eat at my mind, forcing me to recall the one thing I despised and feared the most. It was as if I was lost in another world, forced to come face to face with the beast who was seeking me.

I held my breath as Darcamius' black eyes studied me, and they crinkled with delight at my misery. He laughed and I shuddered, feeling lightheaded. I knew I had to get away from him — he was too close for comfort — but I didn't know how. I could only stare into his hypnotizing eyes, which were luring me further into oblivion.

"Lilianna ..." I heard his menacing voice whisper my name, and it chilled my heart.

I fought to open my eyes, but it was as if I was stuck in some kind of limbo. It was the same as in my nightmare; I was powerless to evade him. Darcamius laughed again, and now his face was only a few inches away from mine. He stuck out his long tongue, and it lengthened, twisting and turning in my face.

"Get away from me!" I screamed, my entire body shaking with fear.

"I've found you, Lilianna ... " he said. *"You will be mine."*

"No!" I shouted. "I will never be yours!"

His features suddenly morphed, and my heart pounded painfully in my chest when I realized I was now face to face with his demonic appearance. Darcamius' black eyes flashed red, and with a cruel smile he leaned in to kiss my lips. I stiffened and squeezed my eyes shut, vomit creeping into my mouth. However, when I tasted the gross liquid, I found it wasn't vomit, but water inside my mouth.

Then Seth's cautious voice drifted through my dream, alerting me out of the unpleasant daze.

"Lily, you're floating near the center! Watch out!"

I opened my eyes and kicked my legs

down at his warning. I tried to swim back towards the bank — but it was too late. The brisk currents pushed me down the river, propelling me into the rushing torrent of the stream. I didn't know what to do, so I simply screamed and flailed my arms at Seth, hoping the half-demon was coming to my rescue.

Seth ran alongside the bank, keeping focused on me as he yelled, "Hang on, Lily! I'll get you out soon! Just stay calm!"

"Seth, I can't!" I yelled back, my heart pounding with fear, but I was slightly relieved when he leapt into the air; his vast black wings emerging. He would rescue me before I drowned.

However, my confidence in surviving the wild waters was hindered when I realized I was being forced farther down the Swift River. There was nothing left for me to do but kick my legs and try to keep my head above the rushing waters, but even that was proving to be difficult. Water was flooding my sight and seeping in through the corners of my mouth.

"Help me, Seth! I can't hold on much longer!" I hollered, finding myself growing weaker with every stroke of my arms.

Suddenly, the currents grew faster, causing my eyes to widen with fright. I closed my mouth as my head bobbed underwater. I kept my eyes closed, but tried my hardest to fight the rapid stream, and as soon as I managed to bring my head above the surface, I drew in a deep breath to fill my empty lungs.

"Lilianna, I'm coming! You're going to be all right! Just try to keep your head above the water!" Seth shouted to me from above. He sounded so convinced, and like a fool I believed him — until I saw the large jagged rocks sticking out of the river, which I was headed straight for.

With a loud squeal, I tried to swim

towards the bank — but I couldn't escape the current. The waters guided me closer to the rocks, and when I was only a few feet away I closed my eyes and braced for impact.

As soon as Seth entered my thoughts, his strong hands grasped my shoulders and hoisted me out of the river. He pulled my wet body into his arms, saving me in the nick of time. It took a few seconds for me to register that I wasn't dead — and that we were now hovering safely above the rushing water. Seth's large black wings flapped steadily as he held me to him, and I glanced up into the eyes of my savior and smiled.

Seth smiled back at me before flying over towards a grassy spot a few feet from the riverbank. He set me down gently into the grass, wiping the wet hair from my face as he stared down at me. I basked in his worried gaze, feeling giddy and lightheaded at the same time. Then my surroundings began to spin and an unsettling chill swept over my body, causing my lips to twitch.

"Lily, are you all right?" Seth asked, still removing the pieces of wet hair stuck to my pale face.

"I'm sorry, Seth," I whispered, gazing up helplessly into his grey eyes. "It was Darcamius. He was in my head and I couldn't...." My throat tightened and I gasped for air frantically, feeling as if I was out of oxygen.

He frowned and shook his head. "Don't speak, Lily. Save your strength."

"I'm cold," I said, my teeth chattering profusely.

Seth noticed my distress and pulled my wet body towards him. He quickly removed his black tee and pressed his bare abdomen against mine. The action felt nice, and all of a sudden I began to feel warmer. I didn't bother inspecting his naked chest though; I was too weak to get excited.

He rubbed his large hands over my frozen arms, eager to warm my shivering body. I tried to smile at him — to thank him for his efforts — but I was too exhausted, and simply gazed up at his anxious expression instead, hoping my eyes would appear grateful. Seth worked faster, trying his hardest to comfort me, and even though he appeared to be calm, I saw the panicked glint in his eyes. I knew that he was still shaken by what had happened.

"You're going to be fine, Lily," Seth said as he wrapped me up in his arms. "I'm going to take you home now."

"Home?" I murmured softly, imagining the bright blue door of my large house and my mother's vegetable garden in the backyard. My mother was smiling at me from the kitchen, whipping up something tasty on the stove while my father read the sports section of the local newspaper at the kitchen table. I smiled at the mental image, yearning to return to that simple, uncomplicated part of my life. How I missed it so.

Seth frowned down at me, drinking me in before he replied sadly, "Yes, Lilianna. Home."

I said nothing. I felt weaker with every breath I took. As I continued to stare up at his face, I found myself slipping away. Seth noticed too and he yelled at me to stay awake — told me not to close my eyes. Then his voice dropped to a low hum, and I could barely understand what he was telling me. I watched helplessly as his lips moved frantically — trying their hardest to keep me awake.

But there was nothing I could do stop the darkness from sucking me into its abyss.

Chapter Eighteen

I arose to the heavenly smell of burnt bacon. My body ached as I came to, and my throat was sore, which I assumed was on account of swallowing gallons of water the day before. I felt lucky to be alive, and as I began counting my blessings, the tray of food sitting on my nightstand caught my eye.

There was a full plate of eggs, bacon, toast, and hash browns resting near my bed, and I knew Seth had prepared them especially for me. I'd told him recently that I loved eggs and bacon. I smiled and reached for the fork on the tray and stuck a hash brown. It was a little cold. It must've been sitting out for some time; nevertheless it tasted wonderful — the best hash brown I'd ever tasted in my entire life. Seth's culinary skills continued to surprise me, and I ate half the plate before my stomach was too stuffed and I gave up. I left the tray on the table and slid out of bed slowly, eager to thank him for the delicious breakfast.

After pulling on a pair of comfortable jeans and my favorite white button down shirt, I wandered down the hall and to the kitchen, where I found Seth sitting at the table and staring listlessly out the window.

"Seth?" I said as I walked up, obviously surprising him out of his train of thought.

Seth seemed shocked and peeved to see me out of bed. His first words to me were, "Go back to sleep, Lilianna. You need rest."

I rolled my eyes at him and crossed my arms. "Good morning to you too—"

"Afternoon," he corrected quickly.

"Whatever. And no, I'm not going back to bed. I'm not tired."

Seth's eyes hardened at my defiance. "You almost drowned, Lily. You're in no condition to be walking about."

"Stop worrying about me. I'm okay," I told him firmly, but I was lying through my teeth. Honestly, I felt a tad lightheaded, but I wasn't going to tell Seth that. He would only fuss over me more. Not wanting him to get another word in on the matter, I wandered over to the couch and sat down, pulling the blanket around my body tightly.

"If you won't go back to sleep, at least stay put on the couch, okay?" He sounded worried, and I couldn't disobey him.

I nodded and leaned back against the back cushion on the couch, closing my eyes as I tried to regain my bearings. After taking a deep breath, I snapped them back open and forced a pretend smile at Seth, who was looking rather anxious.

With a sharp inhale, I said, "Don't look at me like that, Seth. Please. I'm fine."

Seth frowned at me, but he shrugged and replied, "Whatever you say, Lily." He then turned to glance out the window, focusing his attention there.

We sat in silence. Neither one of us attempted to make any form of small talk. I bit my lip nervously, the memory of yesterday's frightful incident chilling my soul. I had almost drowned — I could've died. The only reason I was still sitting here was because of Seth. Once again, he had come to my rescue like a shining white knight. Then I thought that similarity sort of funny. He was more of a dark knight, since he was half-demon.

The silence was eating at me. I knew I had to say something quick, before my mouth started spouting nonsense. I shyly glanced over at Seth's profile, finding him still staring listlessly out the window, and I wondered if I shouldn't disturb him; he seemed so preoccupied by the forest. But I ultimately realized I couldn't hold back what I wanted to say any longer.

After swallowing the giant lump in my throat, I told him what I knew he deserved to hear me say. "Thank you, Seth."

He turned to stare at me, appearing surprised by my gratitude. "For what?"

"For everything," I whispered, giving him a slight smile. "If it wasn't for you, I'd be a corpse right now"

"Lily, you don't have to thank me."

I shook my head at his modesty. "No, I do, Seth. First you saved me from your father, and then those horrible demons. I could've drowned yesterday, but you pulled me out of that river just in time. I keep getting myself in life-threatening predicaments ... I just feel so ashamed."

"Don't blame yourself, Lily."

"How can I not? You've gotten hurt because of me — because of my reckless actions!" I sighed and pushed back my bangs. "You must think I'm such a screw-up."

Seth frowned suddenly and stood up from his chair. He walked over towards the couch and knelt down in front of me. "I don't think that, Lilianna. I could never think that about you."

"Why not? It's true."

With a soft smile, Seth replied, "Because. All humans make mistakes; it's what makes you unique and beautiful. You make mistakes yet you learn from them — and you become a better person in the process."

"Not all humans learn from their mistakes, Seth," I muttered irritably, Marcus coming to mind. "Some just keep screwing up their entire life.

Seth frowned at me and searched my eyes. "True ... but the ones that know they've done wrong and want to do right deserve a second chance. Don't you think?"

I nodded, but not completely agreeing with him. "I guess. But what if I never change? What if I just keep getting myself into danger? What then, Seth?"

"Lilianna, I already told you I will always protect you. Why do you doubt me?"

I blushed from his sweet declaration and asked, "I don't. I just ... I don't know. Nobody has ever been there for me the way you have. No guy has stuck around long enough to take care of me, and I guess it's just a little hard to believe someone will always be looking out for me."

"You don't have to fear me, Lily. Or question my loyalty. I will always be on your side."

"Why do you care so much about what happens to me?" I asked suddenly. "Don't you want to live your own life?"

Seth frowned at me. "A life of loneliness and regret? No, not really."

His response cut into me like a knife.

309

"It doesn't have to be that way, Seth," I whispered.

"Yes it does, Lily."

Seth stood up then and moved towards the fireplace. Leaning up against the mantle, he crossed his arms and dropped his head before adding, "My entire life I have lived on my own. Yes, there have been a few others that I've had the pleasure of knowing, but those people are dead and gone now. The sad reality of my life is that I have no one to share it with. I will forever be alone."

"Don't say that, Seth! It's not true."

His head shot up to glare at me. "Yes it is!" He sighed before adding, "Who in their right mind would want to share their life with a half-demon, Lilianna?"

My eyes welled up at the sight of him in such despair. He was hurting — and it was obvious he hated being alone. He, a powerful demon, needed someone. That was the biggest shock of all. Seth constantly considered himself a monster, but he was far from it. He was more human than he realized.

Seth wasn't like anyone I'd ever met before. Sure, he was a demon, but it was his character that defined him most of all. I'd known plenty of guys in my short lifetime, and many of them weren't nearly as nice to me as Seth has been. They were human, but that didn't make them any better than Seth. Unlike my previous boyfriends and acquaintances, Seth was sensitive, protective, and conscious of his actions. Besides his emotional side, he was strong and powerful, handsome, mysterious … everything a woman could ever hope for in a man. He was a catch, no matter if he had demon blood flowing through his veins. Any girl would be lucky to have a Seth in her life.

A sudden flash of jealousy ignited

within me at the thought of Seth with another girl — looking after her and guarding her the same way he did me. It was obvious I didn't want him to be with somebody else; my face heated up at the mere thought. I peeked over at his distressed face, confusion eating at my mind. These sudden feelings were a complete shock to me. It was as if the blindfold had been removed from my eyes, and I was seeing him for the first time. Seth was special — *how did I overlook that?*

After everything we'd been through together, I should've realized how much he meant to me — and I to him. This was more than just his duty to protect me. Seth cared about me, more than he had ever let on, and I, being the blind idiot, didn't see the love in his eyes. But I saw it now — felt it now, at this sacred moment, as my heart swelled with emotion.

I gathered the courage to tell him the

truth. I was going spill my heart right there in the living room, and I would force him to see that he didn't have to be alone anymore, because I was never going to leave his side again. No matter what, he had me forever.

Recalling his last question had never been answered, I decided to give him a response. "I do," I whispered, shattering the dense quiet.

Seth raised his head slowly and glanced at me, his grey eyes swimming with confusion. "What?"

I wiped at the corners of my eyes and replied, "I want to be with you."

Then I heard it, the boom of thunder and the loud patter of rain falling against the rooftop above my head. Not a good sign.

I bit my lip, trying my hardest to ignore the abrupt change in the weather. "It's true, Seth. As crazy as it sounds, it's true." I smiled, blushing like a grade schoolgirl with a crush. I hadn't been this worked up over a guy in a long time — not even Marcus had made me feel this vulnerable — and that's how I knew my feelings for Seth were true. My giddy heart gave the truth away.

I waited a few moments for Seth to respond, but after an awkward minute of silence, I began to fear the worst. My pulse was pounding as I slid off of the couch and slowly approached him. He stared back at me, the lovely grey of his eyes making me even weaker in the knees.

"I know you're scared, Seth, but you don't have to be."

He shook his head slowly, finally giving me a reaction. "You don't understand, Lily ..."

"I do," I replied hastily. "You're afraid that I won't accept you for what you are — but you're wrong. No matter if you're a demon, I care about you, Seth. I don't care about Darcamius, your powers — any of it! I just want to be with you."

Then the room grew very quiet. Seth gazed down at the floorboards, refusing to look at me, his handsome face hidden behind his long black hair. My breath caught in my throat and I glanced away, feeling foolish for proclaiming my feelings.

"Seth, please say something," I whispered painfully, my eyes welling up on account of his cruel reaction. He couldn't even muster a reply? Any reply would do so long as he acknowledged my feelings — even if he didn't feel the same way as I did.

"So, that's it then? You have nothing to say?" I asked him sharply, my distress turning sour. What was I supposed to do with his silence? My declaration of love had only managed to drive a knife through my heart.

I bit my lip to steady my nerves before

speaking again. "After everything I just told you, Seth ... I don't understand why you won't answer me!" I looked away as I choked up, and I prayed that he didn't notice my sorrow. I didn't want to seem immature, but I figured that was already his opinion of me.

"Lily, there's nothing I can say," Seth replied faintly. His grey eyes were full of anguish, and I knew that he was just as upset as I was, if not more.

I regained my composure quickly, eager to question the reason behind his coldness. "Seth, why—?"

He rushed at me then, grabbing my shoulders fiercely, and my mouth closed from shock. Seth's eyes flashed as they drank me in. I gazed back at him nervously, taken aback by his mesmerizing charm. I cared for nothing but my desire for him at that moment, and my urge to kiss him, but I frowned when I realized he was possibly reading my thoughts. Then Seth dropped his hold on me, and my fears were undeniably confirmed.

"Seth, please don't shut me out," I told him weakly, reaching for his hand.

Seth shook his head and backed away, his black hair falling across his eyes. He retreated to the door of the cabin, but he paused as his hand grasped the knob. Glancing back at me, he said, "I can't do this, Lily. I'm sorry ..." Seth sighed before whispering, "I just can't." He turned away from me then, and without another word, he walked out into the pouring rain.

I bit my lip as I stared after him, fighting back tears. Why was he doing this to me? He felt the same way I did — I was sure of it. That day Seth found me at the springs, he'd been so kind and gentle ... he had rescued me. If he cared, then why was he fighting his feelings for me? I didn't understand him — and I hated him. I hated that he could push me away so easily. I frowned as realization passed through my mind, erasing the anger I'd felt only seconds before. Maybe Seth was pushing me away because he wasn't fully human?

My stomach lurched at the thought, and I suddenly felt sick. Leaning against the broad arm of the couch, I took a few deep breaths to calm myself down. Why didn't I think of that before? It was too easy for me to forget that he was conflicted about his demon side. I exhaled loudly and settled down onto the couch, grabbing a chunk of my hair and tugging it gently. I knew that getting upset over this wouldn't do me any good. Even if Seth wanted to pretend he didn't care about me, I still needed to be strong. I couldn't let this affair of the heart divert me from what was really important.

As I sat there in silence, my traumatic near-death experience from the day before reeled in my head. I had been so sure I was going to die in those rapids, but Seth had been my savior. He'd pulled me out just in time, and had tried to act so strong even though he had really been completely petrified that I'd almost drowned. I smiled, recalling how tightly he had held me in his arms to keep me from freezing. His embrace had felt like something out of a fairytale. It was warm, comforting … no man had ever held me that way before.

I groaned, yearning to feel his arms around me again. When I closed my eyes I heard his voice in my head, remembering what he'd said when he saved me from the river. He'd cradled me in his arms on the riverbank while I slipped in and out of consciousness. I'd barely been able to make out anything that he told me, but I remembered him saying that he'd spent his whole life protecting me, and no matter what happened he was always going to be there to look after me. He also swore that he wasn't going to let his father take me from him.

After a much needed sigh, I fought to remember his last words before I blacked out. They had been important. My pulse quickened as I tried to recall them. I balled my hands into fists and squeezed my eyes shut tightly, trying my hardest to remember. I kept my mind focused on the memory of his voice. *What did he say, Lily? Come on, think!*

Suddenly, a light bulb went off in my head and I heard the forgotten words. I gasped, glancing at the closed door as his voice filled my thoughts. He'd told me he loved me. I remembered it now. Seth had stared down into my eyes, pushing the wet hair off of my face to stroke my cheek when he'd said it.

I lifted a hand to touch the same spot he had caressed as I replayed his soft words over and over again. My heart leapt into my throat with joy and I started shaking, frightened by this turn of events. Seth had actually admitted that he loved me! It was almost too good to be true. But now that I knew how he truly felt, what the hell was I going to do about it?

I didn't give myself enough time to consider my options. Before I knew what I was doing, I was running towards the door, flinging it wide. I stood in the threshold, smiling at his outline in the rain. He was leaning up against a tree, his head propped up by his left hand, and even with his back facing me he was still the most beautiful thing I'd ever seen in my entire life. A streak of lightning lit the sky suddenly, and I grinned, feeling overpowered as I rushed outside into the terrible storm.

Drenched from head to toe, I ignored the heavy rain and my breathlessness as I hurried towards him. "Seth!" I shouted happily.

Seth spun around to face me, surprise covering his face. "What are you doing out here? Go back inside, Lily. You've not fully recovered yet."

The rain cascaded down his face, and he was soaked from top to bottom just as I was. The wet streaks on his face gleamed from the nearby lantern, and I almost gasped from how handsome he looked at that moment. My heart was throbbing profusely as the rain hammered down upon my head, but I welcomed it. With a smile, I advanced on him until we stood only a few feet apart.

Seth frowned, his grey eyes looking me over, and it was obvious he opposed my disobedience. "Lilianna, get back inside!" he said, loudly.

I shook my head and took another step in his direction. "No, Seth. I'm not going anywhere. I'm staying outside with you," I told him, closing the space between us. Glancing up shyly at his beautiful eyes, I resisted the urge to stroke his cheek.

Seth scowled, "Why do you always have to be so damn stubborn, Lily? You almost drowned yesterday! You're in no shape to be—"

"Is that why you told me you loved me? Because I almost drowned?"

Seth studied me closely, his eyes flashing with worry. "What are you talking about?"

I blushed; the truth was written all over his face. "I heard you tell me, Seth," I whispered. "You said you loved me."

He frowned at my admission, and just as he tried to back away from me, I grabbed hold of his hand. He wasn't going to get away from me that easily. Not this time. Seth's eyes widened as I brought his hand up to my cheek, where I nuzzled it tenderly. His expression was adorable, and I knew that he was completely perplexed by

323

such a bold move — especially when it was done by me.

His hand still resting against my cheek, I said, "You don't have to be afraid anymore, Seth. Let me in."

What happened next surprised me. I figured Seth would try to push me away and deny having said anything about loving me, but he did the complete opposite. His stiff posture softened, and without hesitation he brought his other hand to cup my face. My cheeks burned like fire from his touch, and I stared longingly into his conflicted eyes, praying for him to give me a chance. I couldn't bear it if he turned me away again.

The rain was still falling heavily when Seth's hands dropped from my face to wrap around my body. He pulled me close against him, breathing deeply as he held on to my body tightly. I grinned and cuddled into his shoulder, overjoyed by his embrace — but shocked that he hadn't fought me off yet.

To my surprise, Seth lifted one of my hands up to his mouth and kissed each side gently before placing it firmly against his pounding heart. I glanced up at him timidly, butterflies tickling my insides. Standing this close to him, I could scarcely breathe.

Time went absolutely still. The loud sound of the rain faded away to a low patter, and all I could hear was the sound of our breathing. I'm not sure which one of us leaned in first, but either way, our lips collided fiercely. We were both swept up by passion as we held on to each other, kissing and groping like two fools in love. I was trembling as his tongue caressed mine, and I could think of nothing else but returning to the cabin and letting him have his way with me. I wanted more of him — needed more. As his lips lined my neck, he bit me softly, and I cried out his name in ecstasy.

"Oh, Seth — don't stop," I told him, dragging a hand through his soft black hair.

Seth groaned a response before he squeezed my body powerfully. I gasped, feeling crushed, but his grip eased when he realized I couldn't breathe. I grinned with relief and took a deep breath as I slicked my hair back. Seth copied me, and I was forced to tongue him again; he looked incredibly hot with his black hair slicked back.

My jaw dropped from surprise when his hands found my butt, but I matched him kiss for kiss as I allowed him to explore me. A few kisses later, he had already ripped all the buttons from my shirt, and it was wide open, giving him a nice view of my white bra. Man, he worked fast. Seth said nothing as he reached to tug off my shirt, but I cleverly maneuvered myself out of his hold before he had a chance to do so. Flashing him a wide smile, I ran back towards the cabin, eager to get out of the rain and finish what we started where it was nice and dry. As soon as I walked inside the cozy cabin, I found Seth already waiting for me by the fireplace. What a showoff. Leave it to him to try and one up me.

Seth's grey eyes were focused solely on me as he reached for my hand and kicked the door shut, yanking me gently into his arms. In a matter of seconds he managed to rip the shirt from my body, and he threw it carelessly over his shoulder. I gasped as he then fought to remove my bra. As he worked on my bra clasp, I managed to lift his shirt over his head to reveal his well-shaped abdomen. It was glistening from the rain, and I watched mesmerized as a small bead of water traced each crevice until it slipped down into the waistband of his jeans. My God ... I'd never seen a man so perfect.

I bravely placed my palms against his bare chest and smoothed them over his torso slowly — his skin was so soft that I felt compelled to taste it. I licked down his abs affectionately and he trembled. Seth brought my head back up swiftly to take my mouth with his again, and before I knew what was happening, we were both lying on the lush carpet in front of the fireplace.

Sinful thoughts were running through my mind. I wanted him to take me right at that moment, before I got cold feet and came to my senses. Not that I didn't want Seth — I'd been having dirty dreams about him for days, but a dream was just fantasy. This was the real thing ... and it was a big step for me. I'd never had a one night stand before, or sex with someone I wasn't dating, so this was definitely a new experience for me.

After waiting patiently as Seth fumbled with my bra, I realized he couldn't handle the complexity of the clasp and so I undid it for him. I scooted up straight and unhooked my bra, removing both straps slowly before tossing the bra to the floor. Now topless, I shivered and blushed as Seth's bright eyes drank me in.

"You're beautiful, Lily," Seth whispered, and he reached out to stroke me slowly, his hands falling down to cup my breasts. "So beautiful ..." he repeated huskily.

I moaned with bliss from his touch before I lay back down onto the rug, my brown locks pooling around my shoulders. As I watched the firelight dance across Seth's handsome features, I smiled, feeling like the luckiest girl in the world. I couldn't believe that someone like him had chosen me — even if he was part demon. As I looked Seth over, I realized his subspecies didn't deter my feelings for him one bit. I cared for him, no matter what he was.

Seth bent over my body to continue kissing me passionately, and I rubbed up against him eagerly, intoxicated by his nearness. I ran my hands through his black

329

hair, tugging on it gently, and his grey eyes lit up with pleasure. He nibbled my tongue and the action drove me over the edge.

"Seth, I want you," I told him, trembling as he kissed the tops of my breasts. "Make love to me," I whispered, and I took his mouth with my own before he had a chance to answer me.

Seth grunted against my lips and kissed me more roughly, excited by my admission. He pressed his crotch up against my pelvis as he caressed my lips with his, and I could feel how aroused he was, but I flinched when his kisses became almost too rough. Fear flashed through my heart when Seth pinned me firmly against the rug, my head hitting the floor. I tried to ignore the throbbing at the back of my head, but I couldn't disregard his cruel grip. Crying out when my arms flared with pain, I tried to pull away from him, but he refused to let me go.

"Ah ... Seth! You're hurting me!" I told him, stiffening from the pain.

His strength stayed and he seemed absolutely focused, as if he were in a trance. His nails dug into my arm as he sucked on my neck violently, and I bit my lip while forcing back tears as I struggled with him on the floor. His grip eased up and I figured he'd finally acknowledged he was being too rough, but then Seth bit deep into my shoulder and I screamed, his teeth feeling like tiny daggers piercing my skin.

"Seth, stop it!" I yelled, shaking with agony.

His head shot up instantly, and he frowned, looking me over. Seth let go of my arms and I gasped when I noticed that his beautiful grey eyes had turned entirely black. I scooted out from under him quickly and crawled behind the couch to console my pounding heart. What had just happened? I flinched from the pain in my shoulder, and I carefully tried to get a look at the damage. Tears stung my eyes when I noticed his bite-mark was oozing blood. I was trembling, praying for him to come to his senses.

A few minutes passed and he didn't say a word. I managed to calm myself down as I leaned up against the backside of the couch, wrapping my arms around my chest to keep from shivering. Slowly, I crawled to the edge of couch and peeked my head over the side. I found Seth crouched down in the same spot I'd left him. He was staring at the palms of his hands, his black hair hanging in his eyes. I couldn't tell if his eyes had changed back to their usual grey.

I stood up from behind the couch, grabbing his attention. He peered over at me, seemingly shocked by my presence, and his grey eyes were full of grief. Overlooking his pained expression, I smiled, relieved that his demon eyes had vanished.

The terror I'd felt only moments before melted away as I hurried towards him.

"Don't come near me!" he bellowed, and moved out of reach.

I frowned and stopped in my tracks, wary of his harsh tone. "Seth, what's wrong?" I asked softly.

Seth was shaking as he pointed to my shoulder. "I did that to you, Lily … I hurt you." His voice broke off and he looked away, avoiding my eyes. He rose and walked towards the opposite end of the room before adding, "I have to go now."

Confused by his guarded demeanor, I asked, "What? Why?"

"Look at your shoulder, Lily! Why do you think?"

"But it was just an accident, right?" I whispered. Seth didn't answer me, and I frowned, knowing that he was torn up about what he did.

"Seth, you didn't mean to—"

"If I stay here with you tonight, I don't know what I'll do … and I can't take that chance," he interrupted me angrily. "I have to go. It's the only way to keep you safe."

"But—"

"Lily! I'm not going to argue with you about this anymore! Do you understand?"

"Okay …" I said with a nod. Tightening my hold around my chest, I asked him nervously, "Where are you going to go?"

He shook his head and moved towards the front door, reaching for his shirt on the floor. "I don't know …" Seth said as he tugged the shirt over his head. "Somewhere far away from you."

I bit my lip and whispered, "When are you coming back?"

Seth turned away from me, ignoring my question as he opened the door. "Keep the doors locked and the curtains drawn at all times." Twisting his head to glance back at me, he added sternly, "Do not go out into the forest for any reason, Lily. Promise me."

"Seth—"

"Promise me," he repeated hastily.

I swallowed the lump in my throat and whispered, "I promise."

He nodded at me, and just as he was about to walk out the door, I called out to him. "You'll be back soon, right?"

Seth's grey eyes gleamed with distress, but he did not reply as he walked out of the cabin and into the rainstorm. I watched him leave, on the verge of tears. He couldn't leave me all alone like this. It wasn't fair! I ran towards the cabin door, flinging it wide and searching the wet, shadowy forest for him. After a few minutes of scanning the dark wood, I sadly knew he was gone.

I retreated back into the cabin, slamming the door behind me. I locked it and trudged over to the couch, lying down in misery. Seth was gone ... and I had a depressing thought that he wasn't coming back anytime soon. He knew it too, that's why he hadn't answered me when I asked. My shoulder throbbed with pain, snapping me out of my grief, and I carefully reached for the red and grey plaid blanket that hung over the top of the sofa. I draped the soft blanket over my bare shoulders and cuddled into the crease of the couch, careful not to place any pressure on my wound.

Staring up blankly at the ceiling, I wept from loneliness. This was the first time in weeks that Seth and I would be apart, and I didn't think I could handle it. I tugged the blanket off of my shoulder and glanced down at my wound, tracing it delicately as I recalled how close we had been to making love. It had felt so perfect — so right, and I wondered if we would ever try it again.

I studied the bite-mark closely, noticing dried blood caked around it. With a sad sigh, I slid off the couch and wandered over to the kitchen sink, reaching for a rag in the side drawer. After wetting the rag and mixing it with a tiny amount of soap, I brought it gently against the wound and wiped away the blood. I winced, the soap stinging fiercely. Once I was done cleaning away the blood, I stumbled back towards the couch, my heart aching with every step.

I squeezed my eyes tightly as I lay down, pretending it was Seth that I was lying against. It was the only thought that comforted me enough to allow sleep to take me, and I knew I was destined to a place where Seth was waiting for me, even if it was only in my dreams.

Chapter Nineteen

The mansion was prone to creak and moan on windy days, but what could you expect from an old relic like this? It had been abandoned for years and was in definite need of repair; there were holes in the ceiling for heaven's sake. Seth said it was the safest place to hide from his father, but I wasn't so sure. It was hard surviving without electricity and hot water, no matter if a demon was after me or not. I could tell Seth was used to living like this, but I wasn't. Those sorts of conditions are hard on lady, especially one used to the high life.

No matter the tough circumstance though, I was grateful to Seth for his help. He had showed me firsthand what his father was capable of. If he hadn't rescued me from that alley, I would've fallen prey to

Darcamius' sick plans. Thankfully, Seth had intervened just in time and brought me here. I owed him my life and I was going do whatever I could to make it up to him — and to make up for the few punches I gave him when he swooped down and flew off with me over his shoulder.

We'd been shacked up together for over a month, and it took me some time, but I finally got to know the man beneath the demon. He didn't seem dangerous like his father, but it did take me a week or so to warm up to the idea that he was on my side. After all, it was tough enough having to face that fact that demons existed. But Seth had been a gentleman throughout this ordeal. He gave me my space when I asked for it, and answered all of the questions I threw at him. He truly was my dark angel, or so I liked to call him.

This afternoon Seth explained he had a surprise for me, and he seemed really excited about it. I wondered all day what it could be, but I honestly didn't have a clue. Whatever it turned out to be, I knew it would be incredible. Seth hadn't disappointed me once. He brought me bubble bath and even managed to get me caviar when I asked for it. I knew I didn't deserve such special treatment. We were stranded in the middle of Pennsylvania in a decrepit mansion because of me, and Seth's life was put on hold because he was stuck taking care of me too. I felt like such a burden.

Seth insisted I take a bath before he presented me with my grand surprise; he really was thoughtful. After a long, cold soak in the tub, I retired to my bedroom. When I returned to my room, what I found lying on my bed almost brought me to tears. A beautiful gold satin gown, with a pair of matching gold heels, lay unwrinkled on the sheets. I smiled and reached for the dress, absolutely smitten with it. It was exactly something I would've picked out for myself.

I changed quickly, careful enough not to rip the dress. Once I was finished changing, I hurried towards the large mirror in the room. The glass was cracked in two, but I could still see my reflection well enough. I grinned at the sight of my mirror image, which resembled my former self, before I got mixed up with demons. I smoothed my hands over the front of the dress, sighing with longing. How I yearned for my life to return to normal.

There was a knock at my door, startling me from my thoughts. I stared into the sad brown eyes of my reflection, shame washing over me, and I scolded myself for thinking so selfishly. Here I was, alive and well, and wearing a very expensive gown, all on account of Seth. He had done so much for me, and all I ever did was wish that I had never met him. What was wrong with me?

I met him at the door, smiling and thanking him for my present. He was dressed in a black tuxedo, his black hair slicked back, shocking me into a stupor. Once I regained my composure, I told him the gown was a lovely surprise, but he surprised me even more by saying there was something else he had yet to give me. There was more? I didn't know how to react, so I simply took his arm and allowed him to escort me downstairs.

Seth led me down the hall and into the vast ballroom, and there, in the middle of the floor, was a fabulous candlelight dinner. My jaw dropped, and when the shock melted away, all I could do was smile. I grinned up at Seth as he walked me towards the table. He pulled out the chair for me and I sat down without hesitation. I beamed as I looked over the feast he'd prepared. A large, plump duck sat in the middle of the table, surrounded by various sides and two full wine glasses. This had to be the nicest, most romantic thing anyone had ever done for me, and I let him know just that.

He blushed at my compliment and joined me at the table. Before serving the food, Seth took my hand and gave a large speech about how lucky he was to be in my company, even under such morbid circumstances. He then vowed to always keep me safe, and I squeezed his hand, knowing full well that he was earnest. I was confident I could count on Seth to never break his word.

After we finished eating, Seth brought out a record player. Where he found it, I have no idea, but when the jazzy tune drifted from the speaker, my feet began to move with the beat. I could tell by the smile on his face that he knew I loved to dance — but he had followed me from night club to night club for weeks. How could he not?

I grinned and stood from the table, swaying my body to the music. I beckoned Seth to join me, but he was coy and refused. He eventually confessed he didn't know how to dance. I held my hand out to him and pleaded that he take it. I was relentless, and when he moved to obey, a loud boom startled us both. Seth sniffed the air and his eyes turned black; it was at that moment I knew I ought to be afraid.

Seth instructed me to stay indoors while he investigated. I didn't argue with him or ask any questions; I was too scared to speak. I followed his orders and remained in the ballroom for some time, awaiting his return. It was only when I overheard a grotesque grunt echoing from the main hall that I fled the room. I hurried into the kitchen, being careful not to make too much noise. I knew that grunt did not belong to Seth.

I remained low, ducking behind the

large steel island in the center of the room. When loud, clunky footsteps entered the dark kitchen, I held my breath, hoping whoever it was wouldn't detect me. A few minutes passed and I was still unnoticed, the footsteps finally leaving the room. I breathed a sigh of relief and crawled out from behind the island, watching as a large demon retreated back towards the ballroom.

I observed the demon with wide eyes as it sniffed the air, obviously searching for me, and I suppressed a scream when I caught sight of its hideous mug. Two large fangs protruded from its bottom lip; it had red beady eyes hidden behind long black bangs; characteristics similar to that of a man, but mixed with a bull's. I knew I couldn't allow myself to be captured by such a creature.

Remaining low, I hurried out of the kitchen, heading for the open doorway on the opposite end of the room. I fled down the dim hall, lifting my gown as I ran. I had a terrifying feeling that the demon was following me, but I tried to remain positive as I hurried up the stairs. Perhaps once I made it to my bedroom, Seth would come to my rescue. He had to know I was in danger.

After crossing the threshold to my room, I locked the door behind me, moved a large armchair in front of the door, and dragged over the nightstand, hoping it would prevent the demon from getting inside. However, in the back of my mind I knew my efforts were futile. I wasn't dealing with a human being — a demon's strength had to be excessively heightened. If it wanted to come inside, it would find a way.

A large shriek vibrated the quiet walls of the mansion, causing tears to spring to my eyes; the demon was growing closer. I searched around the room, hoping to find some sort of makeshift weapon in case I had to defend myself against the monster.

My eyes fell upon the cracked mirror and I hurried towards it, quickly removing my shoe. I brought the heel against the glass, watching as the crack in the mirror spread. Striking the mirror once more, I grinned with success when a few chunks of glass fell off onto the floor.

I picked up a large shard of glass carefully and walked towards the window. I gazed out at the front of the yard, hoping to locate Seth, and my heart dropped when I saw him lying face down on the ground, a man towering over him with his heel on his head. I pounded at the window fiercely, hoping to distract him, but it was no use. I brought a hand to my heart as I watched the man kick at Seth's motionless form. Suddenly, the door to my bedroom began to crack and splinter as the demon beat at it from the other end, and I hurried from the window.

With a moan of despair, I ran towards

the bed and fell to my knees. I crawled carefully underneath, keeping all of my limbs from sight. Still holding on to the glass, my grip tightened when the door to the room flew off of the hinges and soared across the room. I stifled a scream and squeezed my eyes shut, praying to God to be spared. I was not a religious woman, but if I made it out of this predicament alive, I definitely would pledge my allegiance to God.

I watched the demon's feet walk to and fro, searching every inch of the bedroom, breaking the dresser and the tall bookshelf in the process. It grunted once more, obviously irritated it couldn't find me, and walked towards the bathroom, where I lost sight of it. I exhaled and gripped the glass tighter, ignoring the pain as the glass cut my hand. As I awaited the demon to return to the room, the faint smell of smoke entered my nostrils, causing my pulse to race.

Smoke began filling the room and I gasped, trying to slide out from under the bed. A hand wrapped around my ankle, and I screamed and kicked, but it was no use; the demon had a strong hold on me. Then fire sprang to life in the bedroom, eating everything in its path. I began to cry; the idea of burning alive was too much to bear. The demon released my ankle as it tried to shield itself from the fire, and I crawled out from under the bed, thankful to be free once more.

There was nowhere left for me to turn. The flames were all around me, destroying the room I had called my own for the past month. I screamed in horror as the fire consumed the trail of my dress and spread up the left sight of my body. The pain was great, and I could do nothing but fall to the floor screaming, my body a ball of fire. Eventually the pain was too much for me to withstand, and I took my last breath. Seth was the last thing on my mind before the light went out.

Chapter Twenty

It was raining again. I sighed and lifted my head up off the arm of the couch, glaring at the water slapping against the dirty windowpanes. I thought of Seth and wondered if he was okay. Was he sitting somewhere outside getting soaked? It was all my fault he wasn't here with me right now. I shouldn't have advanced on him like I had. If only I hadn't—

A bead of water plopped onto my forehead, stopping my thoughts. I frowned and glanced at the rickety ceiling above. A few more drops hit my face and I shook my head in exasperation. Great. Now the roof was leaking too? Could my day get any worse?

With a yawn, I stood up from the couch, reaching for the fleece blanket when

I remembered I was still topless. After wrapping the blanket around me like a cloak, I walked to my room and searched through my drawers for a change of clothes. I chose a burgundy button down shirt, a pair of dark jeans, and a black bra and pair of panties. I dressed quickly, careful not to irritate the wound on my shoulder, and stepped back out into the living room. I should've taken a shower, but I didn't care to; there was no one around for me to impress anyway.

The cabin was slightly chilly, and after grabbing a pan to collect the water from the leaky ceiling, I walked over to the fireplace, eager to warm up. I grabbed a few small twigs and tossed them into the pit, setting a few larger logs on top of them. When I lit the match, I watched the fire burn at my fingertips before tossing it against the twigs. The fire ate the wood quickly and I closed my eyes, enjoying the warmth of the flames.

The twisting fire reminded me of my latest nightmare — of Carrine's death. For some reason, compared to Ysmay's and Louisa's fatalities, hers had been the worst to endure. I wondered if it was because she had burned alive, and it had felt so real being trapped underneath that burning bed. The thought of being in the same situation terrified me. I then pondered the idea that it was because of the feelings she'd had for Seth — and how I cared for him too. Out of all three, she was the most relatable reincarnation, and it made the memory so much worse. I couldn't imagine being burned to death while the man I loved fought for my safety, unaware of the pain I suffered.

I thought of Seth, wondering how he lived every day with the guilt of Carrine's death. He had never said it, but I knew he'd loved her just as much as she'd loved him.

It must've been so hard for him. Perhaps that's why he guarded me and kept me so close. If he failed me and I died too, I knew he wouldn't be able to live with the blame.

With a deep breath, I turned away from the fireplace and rose to my feet. After searching the cabin for something constructive to occupy my thoughts, I screamed in frustration when I realized there was nothing but some old books to read. I calmed down eventually, and tried to read the first chapter of a book about a sea captain, but I tossed the book away when I couldn't concentrate. I was too worried about Seth to read anyway. Where had he run off to?

The rain stopped abruptly, distracting my attention, and I raised a brow as the sun shone a bright light into the cabin. I had to shield my eyes, but the ray left as quickly as it had come. *What the Hell?* I peeked curiously out of the window and spotted a head of black hair and grey eyes staring at me from about thirty feet away. Seth? I stared back at the handsome face, trying to identify it.

My heart swelled with excitement. It *was* Seth, standing out in the open. Was he waiting for me? I wasn't sure, but I had to go to him — I just had to. After smoothing down my hair, I went to the front door and opened it. I smiled and rushed out into the forest, enjoying the warmth of the sun against my face and back. Without any hesitation, I hurried over to the spot where I'd found Seth standing only minutes before, but he was nowhere to be found.

I frowned and searched around the quiet forest, hoping to locate him; I found nothing but trees and bushes. He couldn't have gotten too far. *Oh wait. That's right. Seth has wings.* I glanced above me, wondering if he was flying or hiding in a nearby tree. Why would he hide from me?

355

Was he still upset about the bite? I sighed in annoyance and plopped down on a nearby log.

"Seth, please come back to me," I whispered sorrowfully.

All of a sudden, darkness fell upon me. I glanced back at the sky. Clouds had completely blocked out the sun, and the sky was turning a sinister grey. I frowned, feeling uneasy about the murky sky.

A soft wind circled me, chilling me to the bone. I gasped and rubbed my arms vigorously. *What is with this crazy weather?* First it rains, now it's almost pitch-black and it's only four in the afternoon. My heart began to pound. Maybe it wasn't normal ... maybe someone was manipulating it to their advantage.

I inhaled sharply before jumping up off the fallen log. I had to get back to the cabin before something horrible happened. *Seth told me not to leave* ... I had promised him I wouldn't. What was wrong with me? I knew how dangerous it was to leave the safety of the cabin. It's just, when I caught sight of Seth, I — no! I had to focus. Seth wasn't out here. It had been my mind playing tricks on me.

But someone else was in these woods with me — it may not have been Seth, but someone was watching me. I could sense it. That realization made my heart beat faster. As soon as I took a step in the direction of the cabin, the wind turned sharper, pushing against me forcefully. With a scream, I staggered, almost falling over. Not again … please. A low crunching came from behind me, and I turned, my eyes wide with fear. I didn't see anyone, but I didn't want to wait for whoever it was to show up.

Before I gave the stranger a chance to catch up with me, I took off running back towards the cabin. I breathed a sigh of relief when the rickety structure came into view; I thought I was home free. Seth's barrier would prevent any demon from entering it. But when I was only twenty feet away, something strange happened. I grew weaker with every step, as if the air around me was too heavy to breathe.

I tried to keep going but I couldn't, and with a loud cry I collapsed to the ground. Crawling was too much effort, so I simply lay there, my lungs growing heavier with every breath. I cursed myself for being so weak. Then a pair of legs came into my view, and I groaned as I glanced up at the face of Darcamius.

Crouched beside my fallen body, he smiled down at me. I used whatever strength I had to inch away, but Darcamius simply laughed and placed a large hand on the back of my head, holding me firmly in place. My eyes watered from fright when he dipped down to whisper in my ear.

"Did you really think you could hide

from me forever, Lilianna?" he asked, amusement coating his voice.

"No!" I moaned, my hands clawing at the hard earth. "Stay away from me!"

He laughed and stroked my hair. "Lilianna, you poor girl. There's no use in fighting. You're mine now."

I stared back at him in absolute fright. *Seth, where are you?*

Darcamius grinned, delighted by my terror. Then, in a flash, I was in his arms, Darcamius holding me like a small child. His unnatural black eyes bore down into mine menacingly, and with a toothy smile, he asked, "Now, how about that kiss?"

It was the last thing I heard him say before I slipped into unconsciousness.

Chapter Twenty One

The loud sound of gunfire startled me from my sleep. I frowned as I came to my senses, rubbing at my glazed eyes. After I'd fully awakened, I glanced around curiously. I was sitting in an old movie theater. Many chairs missing in the rows, the red wallpaper on the walls was peeling, and a good chunk of the balcony had crumbled off onto the lower level. I glanced to the back of the theater, where the projector was playing an old western on the tattered white movie screen.

My head throbbed painfully as I fought to remember what had happened, and when Darcamius' sinister eyes popped into my mind, I gasped and jumped out of the plush theater seat. *I have to get out of here! Before he—*

I screamed when he leapt down from the balcony above, landing a few rows away. He turned to face me, still in human form, but his coiled horns were protruding from his head.

"Lilianna, you're awake. Excellent," he said with a large smile. "It looks like we can finally finish what we started all those years ago."

I sidestepped down the row of empty chairs, eager to get to the main aisle before he grabbed me. I knew what he wanted from me — but there was no way I was going to have sex with that monster. He would have to kill me first.

"Stay away from me!" I yelled as I ran out of the row. I turned to run up the aisle, but Darcamius leapt into the air and cut me off. His jump was so powerful it cracked the floor beneath his feet.

I gasped and staggered backwards, holding up my fingers to make a cross.

Darcamius chuckled at me and shook his head. "You are so amusing, Lilianna. Do you really think that's going to work?"

I trembled at his question but still held up my fingers.

He laughed some more and began to walk towards me, his grey eyes turning black.   My heart was pounding in my ribcage. I would be letting the brave women who'd come before me down if I allowed him to take me. I would try to stop him until there was no more breath left in my body.

I glanced left and right as I backed down the main aisle, searching for some type of weapon to defend myself, but there was nothing but dust and debris from the walls. As I was about to give up hope, I saw a broken piece of metal lying at the beginning of one of the aisles. After swallowing the lump in my throat, I made a dash for it, and I exhaled with relief when I grasped it in my hands.

Darcamius raised his brows at me, an amused expression on his face. "What do you plan on doing with that, Lilianna?" he asked with an angry tone. "Put that thing down before you hurt yourself."

I held my weapon out in front of me. Who was I kidding? I couldn't fight Darcamius. He was a demon lord. The best chance I had was if Seth swooped down from the sky and came to my rescue. But he wouldn't. He didn't even know where I was.

That realization brought tears to my eyes, and for a split second I was vulnerable — but that second was all Darcamius needed to blindside me. Before I knew what happened, he was standing directly behind me, snaking his right arm around my belly.

"No!" I screamed, kicking my legs as he hoisted me up with one arm.

"I know you're frightened, Lily ... but you don't have to be. Just accept your fate," Darcamius murmured, before leaping into the air. My stomach lurched from the intensity of the jump, and I kept my eyes closed tightly until he landed on the second level of the theater.

Darcamius lowered me to the ground slowly, and I struggled to breathe as I cowered on the floor of the balcony. Without warning, he grabbed my ankles and pulled; I tried clawing at the ground, but it was no use. I screamed as he dragged me over to an odd circle full of blankets and pillows. Tall white candles formed a ring around the bed, and with the flick of his hand, Darcamius set them all alight.

I moaned in agony when Darcamius laid me gently onto my back, and as soon as his hands moved to unbutton my blouse, anger crept up my throat.

"Get your hands off of me!" I yelled at him anxiously, tears filling my eyes. I couldn't let this happen. I tried to sit up, but Darcamius pushed me back down atop the plush blankets, pinning me with one hand.

"Lily, Lily, Lily ..." he began, shaking his head. "Do not fight me. It will only infuriate me. You don't want to infuriate me, now do you?"

Tears rolled down my face as I stared into his evil black eyes. "Please, don't ..." my voice caught in my throat and I almost choked. I was hyperventilating.

"Hush now," he whispered lustfully, using his free hand to finish undoing my buttons. Darcamius groaned at the sight of my bare flesh, and I watched in horror as he lifted the same hand into air, the nail of his index finger growing into a sharp black claw. He flashed a menacing smile at me, and with a swift stroke of his finger, he cut the skin beneath my bra.

I cried out from the pain. It was excruciating, and my eyes grew wide with fright when I felt a small trail of blood trickle down my waist. The sight of my blood caused Darcamius' black eyes to enlarge, and after a loud sigh escaped his throat, he lowered his head to lap at my oozing wound, his eyes rolling back into his head.

I felt completely helpless as Darcamius consumed my blood. I couldn't defend myself against him — he was too strong. How could this be happening? Seth swore he wouldn't allow his father to lay a finger on me. *He promised he would always protect me!* I cried harder at the thought that he had broken his word.

"Seth!" I screamed through my tears, writhing against Darcamius' mouth. "Seth, where are you?" I murmured weakly.

"He'll never find you," Darcamius answered, raising his head to stare at me, and I flinched in fear when I noticed his bloodstained lips. He smiled at my distress, and before I could turn my head, Darcamius pressed his mouth firmly against mine. As he forced his tongue down my throat, the demon lord grabbed breasts, squeezing them tightly.

His kiss was overpowering, and I almost fainted from the taste of my blood.

He removed his lips from mine to whisper huskily, "You're mine now, Lilianna. No one will ever separate us again."

"You're delusional!" I spat, blood and spit flying at his face. "I will never be yours!"

"We'll see about that," he replied, standing.

I shook with fear as I awaited Darcamius' next move. He hovered above me, staring deeply into my eyes, his grey eyes now turning black. When he moved to unbutton my jeans, his features began to change to the same demonic beast from my nightmare.

"No," I cried, my heart racing.

As Darcamius laced his fingers through

my belt loops, the ceiling above our heads cracked. We glanced up at it, startled by the sound. I watched the crack spread, and when I glanced at Darcamius, I noticed his mouth lifting into a toothy grin.

His full transformation was put on hold, but I gasped at the sight of his elongated fangs and tried to inch away from him. Darcamius was aware of my withdrawal, and before I had a chance to run away, he turned to glare at me. I was mesmerized by his large eyes, watching them flash a bright red. When he stood, I found I was frozen to the spot.

Just then, the ceiling broke through, and down came Septhim — along with age-old roofing and cement. He landed in a perfect crouch, dust and debris coating his entire body. Without a word, Seth slowly stood out of the dust cloud, his head bowed as he stared his father down in anger.

Darcamius' back was turned towards

me, but I watched him shake his head back and forth as he laughed.

"So nice of you to join us, Septhim. Better late than never, son."

Seth took a short step towards him. He peeked over Darcamius' shoulder to find me lying in the circle of his father's sin.

"Everything is going to be all right, Lilianna," he told me firmly. "You're safe now."

Darcamius chuckled louder at Seth's hopeful comment. "Don't lie to the poor girl, Septhim. Her fate was sealed a long time ago — as was yours, when I laid with your human mother."

Seth began to shake; his hands at his side balled into fists. He looked absolutely furious, and I feared his actions. I wanted to go to him — to kiss him just in case it was the last time I would ever get the chance to. But I still couldn't move.

"You're weak, Septhim," Darcamius

declared haughtily as he approached my petrified body. "You're no match for my power." He lifted me carelessly up off of the ground, and as he raised me high into the air, his nails began to dig into my skin. I wanted to cry out from the pain — but I could only stare anxiously at Seth.

"Do you want her, *Seth?*" Darcamius taunted, dangling me in front of him like candy. "Then come and get her!"

Without warning Seth began to charge, his grey eyes on fire. Darcamius laughed and tossed me to the ground, leaping out of Seth's way. I collided with the floor, my left shoulder aching with the impact. Even now I couldn't rise.

Darcamius shoved his shoulder into Seth's side, propelling him far across the room until he hit the stiff brick wall behind him and sprang to his feet uninjured. In a flash, Darcamius rushed at him again, his large claws extended. I watched in complete awe as with each strike Seth received from his father, I thought the worst. But he got right back up and returned the blows, surprising me — and even Darcamius. His half-demon son wasn't going down without a fight.

Then Darcamius decided to play dirty. He raised his right hand and set it aflame, pointing it at the ground beneath Seth's feet. With a wicked grunt, he shot a fireball from his hands, but Seth dodged it by vaulting into the air, his wings emerging instantaneously. I stared wide-eyed at his vast black wings, and hopefulness rushed through me. Maybe he could beat Darcamius after all. He had wings, unlike his father, and could use them to his advantage.

"That's right. I almost forgot about your precious wings, Septhim," Darcamius said, after raising his other hand. He held both of his large hands out in front of him now, and I saw a sort of uncertainty in his eyes.

"What's wrong, Father? Are you scared of them?"

"Don't be absurd," Darcamius replied with a growl, his voice deepening.

With a menacing grin, Darcamius' left hand released a fireball, followed closely by his right, until they discharged almost repetitively. Seth dodged them with ease, but the structure of the theater did not, and in a matter of seconds the far end of the balcony was ablaze.

I eyed the twisting flames with dread. I still couldn't move. I glanced anxiously at Seth, who was utterly focused on the ongoing battle with his father. It was sort of ironic that while battling over me, they both had forgotten about me.

"You seem to have lost your touch, Dad," Seth told him arrogantly, flapping his wings violently.

"Your maneuvers are impressive, son. But you're fighting a losing battle. You and I both know that by the end of this, you're going to be the one lying in a pool of your half-breed blood!"

"We'll see about that, Darcamius!" With a loud grunt, Seth swooped down at his father, gripping his right arm and lifting him up into the air. He tossed Darcamius against the wall roughly, but the demon rose unscathed, only a small trail of blood creeping out from the corner of his mouth. Darcamius glared at his son, obviously angered that he was bleeding, and shot another fireball. This time it was bigger — a lot bigger — and Seth couldn't dodge it.

I watched in horror as the blast consumed Seth, setting the wall behind him on fire. No ... *Seth* ... my eyes welled up at the sight of his body lying face-down on the floor of the balcony, smoke rising from his back.

"Like I said ... weak," the demon lord said with a smirk, wiping the corner of his mouth. He strolled over towards Seth's limp body, and I burned with rage when he towered over him. Seth was motionless and I feared the worst. He had to be okay — he just had to be!

"I didn't want to kill you, Seth. But I'm afraid I have no choice." He glanced in my direction and smiled, his black eyes frightening me. "You're going to watch me rip him in half, Lilianna. After that, we'll finish what we started."

I closed my eyes tightly, trying to find some sort of strength within myself. I had to help Seth. *He won't die because of me. I won't stand for it!*

All of a sudden, a bright blue light shone down at me, filling me with an intense feeling of tranquility. I sighed, tilting my head back as the alien force rushed through my entire body. It felt like a thousand tiny kisses caressing my soul, and when I saw the face of the culprit, I smiled. A small woman, with six feathery white wings attached to her body, smiled back as she hovered above me. She placed a warm hand on my forehead and stared deeply into my eyes. Time seemed to stand still, and I knew in the pit of my stomach that she was a divine force.

When I blinked, the winged creature and the light vanished, but I felt a strong energy trying to push its way out of my chest. My hands balled into fists as the energy placed an intense pressure on my body, but the pressure was too much for me to bear and I screamed. Immediately after my scream, the energy escaped, breaking the invisible binds that were snaked around my body.

I gasped for air, unsure of what had just happened, but I knew I didn't have time to second guess my chance at freedom.

Overwhelmed and weak, I rose to my feet, staggering towards Darcamius and Seth. No matter what Darcamius did to me, I was not going to stand idly by while he tortured Seth. I didn't know what I could do to stop him; all I knew was that I had to try.

"Leave him alone!" I shouted at the mighty demon lord. I was shaking with fear, but I hid it the best I could; I wasn't going to give him the satisfaction. "I'm the one you want — not Seth."

Darcamius seemed surprised to hear my voice. He twisted his head around and he smirked, amused to find me on my feet. "How did you manage to get free of my curse, Lilianna, hmm?" His black eyes flashed red once more, but they had no effect on me this time. With a frown, he retreated from Seth's side and headed in my direction.

"What's this?" After studying me for a moment, he gasped and lifted his arms to shield his eyes. "That blue light!" he growled. "Damn those saints!"

I took a step toward him, bringing up my hands. I shut my eyes and lifted my arms high above my head. Suddenly, I felt the energy release around me, and when I opened my eyes, I was standing in a bright blue bubble. I smiled, the bubble emitting a warm, safe sensation.

Darcamius growled and leapt at me, his black claws outstretched. When he collided with the force field, he ricocheted backward, crashing into the ledge of the balcony. Large pieces of cement crumbled down onto the lower level as Darcamius vaulted to his feet, his face now twisted with madness.

"This isn't possible! They can't interfere!" he hissed, squeezing his fists tightly. "It's against the rules!"

The demon lord approached me once more, keeping a foot of distance between himself and the blue barrier. I watched in fear as his black eyes grew larger, his stature lengthening. Darcamius' handsome façade dissolved into a more frightening look — his true form. He was now the same beast from my nightmare.

My pulse quickened with horror at the sight of his monstrous appearance, but I still held my ground. I thought of Ysmay, Louisa, and Carrine — and it gave me the strength I needed to stand tall. I wasn't going to stand by and let him have his way with me; I would fight him until I had no more strength.

"It's useless, Lilianna. You are *mine!*" he declared with a deep shriek. When Darcamius lifted his large, dark hands to strike the barrier, I braced myself. I hoped it was strong enough to withstand his evil power.

"No, she isn't," Seth replied loudly, gaining our attention. As he struggled to stand, Seth added, "She was never yours!"

I beamed at the sight of him. "Seth! Thank God you're okay!" I said with a warm smile.

He smiled weakly at me before confronting his father. "You will not touch another hair on her head!" Seth shouted.

Darcamius snorted and tossed back his black hair before he lunged at his son, and the two demons began to brawl once more. They kept clear of my bright barrier, and fought towards the opposite end of the balcony, where the flames were still thriving. I eyed the fire nervously, watching as it ate the walls of the old theatre. When it began to spread towards me, I figured it was time to get to safety.

With one last look at Seth, I ran towards the stairwell, hurrying to the lower level. I bounded down the stairs in a matter of seconds and rushed out into the main aisle. The barrier around me suddenly

vanished, but I could still feel the power
rushing through my body. I craned my head
to gaze up at the balcony, focusing solely on
Seth's wellbeing. I gasped as I watched the
fire spread towards Seth and his father, my
heart trembling with panic.

"Seth, the fire! Watch out!" I shouted.

When Seth turned to acknowledge me,
Darcamius slammed into him. I watched in
horror as Seth fell off of the balcony at a
rate so fast it caused my brain to whirl. He
crashed into a row of empty red seats and
they collapsed from the force of his impact.
After the dust settled and I could see
clearly, I realized he wasn't moving.

"Seth!" I shouted, running towards
him, hurdling over debris. I knelt down
beside his fallen body, gasping at the
bruises and cuts along his jaw and cheeks.
Darcamius had really done a number on
him. My hair fell in my eyes as I bowed my
head — hiding my misty eyes. I groaned

from despair and laid my head gently on his chest.

"Seth, please," I whispered, stroking his arms. "You have to wake up."

He didn't move. I didn't even think he was breathing. I studied his relaxed face, tears streaming down my cheeks when I dipped my head towards his. He couldn't be dead … he just couldn't be. Despair coated my heart, and it was at that moment when all hope was lost that something dawned on me, and I didn't understand how I could've missed it before. As I stared down at Seth's expressionless face, I realized I was hopelessly in love with him.

My eyes seeped tears as I looked Seth over, but I smiled, feeling happy to finally understand the depth of my devotion for him. "I love you, Seth. Please … wake up," I whispered, before bringing my lips against his. I kissed him softly, savoring the taste of his tender mouth. I remained this way for a few moments until I realized it wasn't working. He wasn't waking up. This wasn't a fairytale; true love's kiss wouldn't revive him. I choked on my tears and drew back, staring sadly at his listless face.

I heard footsteps approaching me, and I frowned, and tossed a glance over my shoulder. Darcamius sneered down at me, shaking his head before grasping my arm and pulling me to my feet.

"You've got passion in you, Lilianna," he told me huskily. "Much more than the women before you. I kind of like it."

"Take your hands off of me!" I told him angrily, while trying to wrestle out of his fierce grip. "Let me go!"

Darcamius squeezed my arm tighter and replied, "There's no need to shout." Tossing me over his shoulder rudely, he added, "Come now. It's time to finish what we started those many years ago."

"No!" I hollered, kicking my legs and

flailing my arms. I glanced back at Seth desperately, hoping he would wake up. "Seth, help me! Please!" I whimpered with despair when he didn't move.

This was it. Darcamius would finally plant his demonic seed. I would be forced to endure the pain and suffering of his forced love-making. I closed my eyes tightly, ignoring the tears sliding down the sides of my face. But I realized I didn't care about falling prey to this monster's obsession — or the fact that I had been through hell to prevent this moment for ever happening. All I could think about was Seth.

Seth, who was lying unconscious on the cold, dusty floor of the decaying theatre. All because of me. This half-demon had risked everything to keep me safe ... and I loved him for it. I loved him with my entire heart. He wasn't going to die, not on my watch — and when I opened my eyes, I knew what I had to do.

I used whatever power I still possessed from the divine being to aid me in leaping off of Darcamius' shoulder. I hurried back to Seth, ignoring the demon lord's loud roar of disapproval. My hands were shaking as I bent over Seth's cold body and lowered my head until our noses touched. Just one more kiss ...

I wasted not another moment. I closed my eyes and searched my soul for the strange power, and when that familiar energy tickled my insides, I knew I had found it once again. I grinned as the serene sensation passed over me and I focused the energy solely into my lips. As I kissed Seth tenderly, I prayed for him to be spared. I chose not to use this power to destroy Darcamius, but to spare his son — the man I loved. Hope rushed through me, and as soon as the kiss ended I raised my head to see if it had worked. I cried with joy when I found his grey eyes staring up at me.

"Lilianna," Seth murmured, lifting a hand to stroke my cheek. "You saved me."

"I had to," I whispered back, my heart bursting with joy. I couldn't believe it. Seth was alive! I had actually brought him back. I silently thanked the celestial powers above for their help, before wrapping my arms around him tightly.

"I'm so glad you're all right. I was so worried you were—" My voice cracked and I gripped his hand tightly. "Don't ever scare me like that again."

His grey eyes softened and he nodded. "I won't, Lily. Thank you."

I smiled at him, and just as I was about to kiss his lips again, I was yanked into the air. Darcamius threw me halfway across the room and I hit the ground with a considerable amount of force. My entire body flared with pain and I groaned as I tried to stand — but I felt too weak to move. I simply laid there until Darcamius' legs came into view.

"How dare you!" he screeched, foaming at the mouth. "You belong to me!"

I watched Darcamius bare his fangs as he lifted me up once more; he shook me violently, rage etched across his face. I stared into his black eyes, feeling faint. I couldn't even breathe. Suddenly, a bright light exploded in the room, flashing in every direction. Darcamius' hold on me faltered as he used his free hand to shield his eyes.

"Put her down, Darcamius," Seth stated firmly. "Now."

When I glanced in Seth's direction, I was surprised to find him shrouded in a bright blue light — the same light bestowed to me from the seraph.

"That can't be! You're a demon — that sort of divine power should kill you instantly!" Darcamius objected, trembling with uncertainty. He dropped me carelessly before facing his son once more. "How can you withstand their untainted force?"

Seth narrowed his grey eyes at Darcamius before saying, "I may be half-demon, but I'm nothing like you, father. I'm not evil."

With the slash of his hand, a blue, razor-like beam released off of his fingertips — striking Darcamius in the middle of the chest. He howled and staggered backward, eyeing his chest in fear. My jaw dropped at the sight of the deep gash in his midsection, surprised by the sheer intensity of his blow.

Seth didn't stop there. Using the pure blue energy to form a giant sword, he leapt into the air and plunged it straight down into his father's shoulder. Darcamius howled with rage, and as he fought to resist, the blue energy consumed his body, incinerating him in a matter of seconds. I stared fearfully down at the pile of ash where Darcamius had previously stood, wondering if it had really worked — if the evil demon was actually gone.

Seth groaned and staggered backwards, the divine energy vanishing from his clutches. I ran to his side and wrapped my arms around him to keep him on his feet. He leaned into me, kissing the top of my head as he eyed the remains of his father.

"It's over," Seth whispered incredulously. "It's really over."

"Are you sure he can't come back?" I asked, yearning to hear the truth.

Seth's shocked expression melted into a smile as he said, "No. He was destroyed by the divine light. Darcamius can never come back. He's gone." I smiled and hugged him to me, the dread in the back of my mind finally dissolving. It really was over. Darcamius was dead, and I didn't have to hide in fear that he would take me away again. I could go back to the life I had missed so much. I could finally start living again.

After giving my shoulder a reassuring squeeze, Seth smiled and said, "Come on, Lilianna. It's time you went home."

I smiled up at him and nodded. "You read my mind, Seth."

We walked side by side out of the decaying theater, Seth's right arm wrapped tightly around my shoulders. I leaned into him, relief washing over me. It was finally finished — this age-old obsession. Darcamius wasn't going to hurt me, or anyone else ever again.

Chapter Twenty Two

We pulled up in front of my house at eight minutes past dawn. I'd been asleep almost the entire car ride home; not even the bumps in the road had awakened me. The battle with Darcamius had worn me out. I glanced over at Seth, wondering where he found the strength to drive all night across New Hampshire.

I frowned, feeling foolish for even pondering such a thing. Seth wasn't human. It always amazed me that such a big and serious detail could escape my mind so easily. He didn't operate the way humans did; he barely needed sleep, if any. After bunking with him in that cabin for weeks, I should've remembered that.

Seth had snagged a car parked near the theater, unlocking it with his nail. I felt sort of guilty for stealing someone's car, but it was exhilarating nonetheless. Besides, I needed the rest and didn't care about anyone else's misfortune at the moment. Which is exactly why Seth stole a car instead of flying me home. He knew I needed a few hours to recover before I met up with my parents.

Before leaving he dialed 911, alerting the authorities that the movie theater was on fire, but that there was no one inside. It was still burning brightly when we drove away, and the thought that Darcamius' ashes were burning with it brought me nothing but satisfaction and relief. The nightmare was over for good.

Seth drove down my street slowly and parked in front of my neighbor's house. When his hands dropped from the steering wheel, I peeked over at him. He dipped his head down to stare at his lap, and his dark locks fell over his eyes. I wanted to reach out to him. We hadn't spoken since the battle, and I was afraid of what he was thinking. Our last conversation before his father showed up had been less than pleasant, and I feared the worst. Was he really going to abandon me and run off?

"Thank you," I told him, ending the uncomfortable silence between us. When he didn't respond, I tucked a chunk of my hair behind my ear and added, "If it hadn't been for you, Seth, I would've—"

He held up his hand and nodded, interrupting me. "It's alright, Lilianna. You don't have to thank me."

"But I do," I whispered.

Seth glanced over at me and smiled. "It's not necessary." Without another word, he opened the driver's side and stepped out of the car, motioning for me to do the same. "Come on, your parents have to be worried sick about you."

I nodded and stepped out, shutting the

door behind me gently. As I followed him down the sidewalk and up my driveway, I bit the inside of my cheek, fishing for the right words to say. What Seth did for me was amazing. I owed him my life ... and my heart. He told me not to mention what had happened that night before his father captured me, but I didn't think I could forget about what had happened between us. I didn't think he could either.

"Well, I guess this is it," Seth said, eyeing me closely.

I frowned, unsure by what he meant. "What—?" But I closed my mouth when my father came into view.

He ran off of the porch at full speed, headed straight for us. I beamed at the sight of him. How much I missed him and the rest of my family. I searched the porch for my mother, hoping she was just as eager to see me. Then, out of nowhere, I saw her hurrying after my dad, her eyes wide with worry. They met us halfway, my mother bursting into tears.

"Lily! Lily, honey ... is that you?" I smiled and let her wrap me up in her arms.

"Hi, Mom," I whispered faintly, enjoying the warmth of her hug.

"My little girl," she cooed, hugging me tighter. "Is it really you? "

I smiled and hugged her back. "Yes, Mom. I'm back."

She began to cry even harder. "Do you have any idea how worried we've been, Lilianna? We thought ..."

I nodded and glanced back at Seth, noticing his troubled expression. "I know, Mom. I'm sorry."

"Who's this?" she asked me softly. My mother eyed Seth with an odd look on her face, as if she couldn't comprehend why he was there.

"This is Seth, Mom," I said, smiling over in his direction. "He saved my life."

My mom's confused look brightened as she studied him. "He did? How?"

I nodded. "Yes, he did ... but it's a very, very long story. I'll tell you and Dad all about it later."

My mother frowned, but kissed my cheek tenderly and replied, "All right, Lily. Why don't you two come inside now, I'll whip up something for you to eat."

"Okay."

As Seth was about to join my side, my father stepped deliberately in his path. He crossed his arms and surveyed him with a disgusted expression.

"Who are you?" Dad asked him angrily. "You're the reason Lily has been gone, aren't you?" My dad looked so furious; his neck and face were bright red, his eyes were almost bulging out of his sockets. I feared for Seth, but when I tried to get between them, my father yelled at me to stay back.

"Dad, please—"

My father ignored my plea and continued to stare daggers at Seth, who looked considerably cool at the moment. "I asked you a question, young man. Who are you, and where did you take my daughter?"

Seth met my dad's eyes bravely, and with a bow of his head, he replied, "My name is Seth, and yes, I did take your daughter away for a while. But I had to — she was in danger. If I hadn't intervened, and left her here with you, she would have died."

Dad's furious expression melted away into a confused look. "What are you talking about? Why was she in danger?"

"I'll tell you why, Dad," I spoke up suddenly, walking around him and standing by Seth's side. "But later, please. I just got home." I gave him my trademark pout, and that usually would do the trick whenever I wanted something. I wasn't sure it would work now, though. My father looked stark-raving mad.

He frowned suddenly and shook his head, the red flush draining from his face. "All right. I'll let it go for now."

"Thanks, Daddy," I replied with a relieved smile, and walked over to give him a hug.

He hugged me back and stroked my hair gently. After kissing the top of my head, he said, "I'm just glad you're home."

"Me too …" I whispered.

"Come on," my father said, taking my right hand in his. "A lot has happened since you've been gone."

My mother placed her arm around my left shoulder then, and the three of us walked up the brick path to my back porch. When we reached the sliding glass doors of my house, I realized Seth wasn't with us. My parents opened the door and stepped inside, but I froze in the threshold, glancing

behind me. He wasn't there — or anywhere.
How could that be? I hadn't heard him
leave.

I searched my backyard frantically,
wondering where Seth had run off to. He
couldn't have gotten far; he had been
standing right beside me only a second ago.
My eyes grew misty as I investigated the
backyard, but my heart raced with joy when
I noticed a black head moving swiftly
through the trees in the woods behind my
house. I glanced at my parents, and they
both were watching me with anxious
expressions.

"Lily? What's the matter?" my mother
asked me.

I frowned at her, then glanced back at
Seth's disappearing head. I couldn't just
stand there — I had to go after him. I would
regret it if I didn't.

"I'm sorry ..." I said softly, turning to
face my parents again. There were tears in

my eyes, and the sight of them caused my mother to frown.

"Why? Honey, what is the matter with you?" My mother stepped out of the house, but I backed away from her and turned to run.

"Seth! Wait for me!" I cried out, before rushing off of the deck and hurrying after him.

"Lilianna! Come back here!" my father yelled, but I ignored him and kept running.

Tears were streaming down my face, and I must've looked downright horrible ... but I didn't care. I had to tell Seth how I felt before he disappeared from my life forever. This was the only chance I had, and I wasn't going to let it pass me by. Seth was the most amazing person I'd ever met, and he deserved to be loved — no matter if he was human or not.

When I reached the forest behind my house, my heartbeat quickened, and I felt breathless when I caught sight of my half-demon wandering amongst the tall trees. His long black hair hung in his eyes, his head bowed as he walked. I could tell by his stance that he was just as upset as I was that he was running away.

"Seth!" I yelled, picking up my pace. He didn't hear me though — I was too far away. He kept on walking, until he disappeared amongst the trees. I groaned and ran faster, ignoring the stinging pain in my side as I prayed not to lose him. If I did, I knew I would never see him again.

I hurdled over a few large rocks, racing down the faded trail through the woods behind my house. The woods were familiar to me — I had played in them many times as a child — and I was confident I would be able to find him. When a clearing came into view, I spotted him. He was leaning against a tree, staring up at the sky. I looked up too, wondering what he was staring at, but there was nothing but clouds and treetops above our heads.

When I walked closer towards him, my foot snapped a small branch on the ground, the sound alerting him. Seth twisted his head in my direction and his dark brows furrowed with anger when he found me standing there.

"What are you doing here, Lily?" Seth asked, pushing off of the trunk with his foot. "I told you that I can't—"

"That you can't be with me? I know. But I don't care, Seth. I love you."

Seth's grey eyes flashed with grief and he glanced down at his feet. "Lily, please. Don't do this."

"Do what?" I asked breathlessly. "Love you with all of my heart? It's too late for that, Seth. I already do — and you know that!"

He frowned at me and replied, "Lily, will you please just—"

"No," I interrupted firmly, walking near him, but I kept a foot of distance between us. I gazed up into his eyes helplessly and said, "I've listened to you for weeks, Seth. I've done what you said! Now it's your turn to listen to me."

Seth's tense expression disappeared, and after studying me for a moment, he nodded slightly and said, "All right, Lily. You win."

With a triumphant sigh, I reached out my right hand to stroke his soft cheek. I hesitated before touching him, afraid he would smack my hand away. He didn't though, and with a smile I slowly caressed his face. I placed my hand gently on his shoulder just as he lifted his hand to sift it through my hair. I relished the feeling, enjoying the tender way he stroked my hair.

"I've never felt this way about anybody my whole life," I told him softly.

"Neither have I," he whispered back,

bowing his head closer to mine.

I grinned and added, "You're amazing." I paused to rest my free hand on his other shoulder. After wrapping both my arms around his neck, I said, "I don't care if you're a half demon, Seth. It doesn't matter to me one bit."

Seth's head shot up. I frowned when I noticed he was glaring at me.

"It should matter to you, Lilianna. I'm not human!" he shouted loudly, removing my hands from his body. He stepped away from me to say, "You need to forget about me. I'm no good for you."

"Stop it! Stop punishing yourself for something that isn't your fault. You saved my life, Seth. You're a good person."

He shook his head and replied, "No. I'm a demon."

"A part of you is human!" I countered loudly.

Seth crossed his arms and shot back,

"And the other part isn't, Lily! It never will be." He looked me over before saying, "How can you expect me to love you when I can't even love myself?"

I frowned, knowing how much he hated his demonic half. But it didn't bother me one bit. So what if he was a demon? He was still a man — and a good one at that. That was all that mattered. Why couldn't he see how amazing he truly was?

"There are things about me, Lily that you don't know. Things I've done—" His voice fell and he looked off, his grey eyes welling up with tears.

"That doesn't matter to me," I told him, shocked by the distressed look on his face. "The past is in the past for a reason, Seth. Didn't you tell me you believed in giving people second chances? Well this is your chance to start over. With me."

Seth frowned, refusing to look at me as he stared at the ground beneath my feet.

"You're wrong. I don't deserve a second chance."

"What is it going to take for me to get through to you?" I whispered faintly.

My cheeks flushed when remembering our kiss the night before his father captured me. The way Seth touched me and held me … as if I was destined to be in his arms forever. I couldn't survive without him. I'd never felt this way with anybody else. How could I just abandon that feeling? How could he?

"Seth, I need you," I murmured, closing the space between us. Before he could object, I boldly placed my arms around him and laid my head against his shoulder. I breathed in his scent, relishing his unique smell, and I felt the tears threatening to fall at the idea that this would be the last time I would hold him. He couldn't leave me. He'd promised he would always be around to protect me.

Seth accepted my hug and held me against his body tightly. His embrace was warm and tender, and I nuzzled my face into his chest. When I glanced up at him, his eyes bore down into mine and I grew breathless from their intense look. Before I knew what happened, Seth kissed me. I smiled against his lips and kissed him back, my grip on his body tighter. We stayed that way for what seemed like eternity — until Seth pulled back to grace my cheek with a kiss.

"You love me," I whispered happily, kissing his lips again. "You can't deny it."

He closed his eyes tightly, and bumped my forehead with his. "I've always loved you, Lilianna," he whispered softly. After kissing the top of my head, he added, "I've loved you for hundreds of years ... and I will continue to love you for the rest of my existence."

I melted at his statement and took his

hands in mine. "Why wouldn't you tell me how you felt before, Seth?"

"Because ..." he replied sadly. "It doesn't change anything."

My heart dropped. "How can you say that? Of course it does!"

Seth's grey eyes darkened. "No, I'm afraid it doesn't."

"What?" I felt as if the wind had been knocked out of me. "Why are you saying these horrible things?"

"Because, Lily," he began quietly, removing his hands from my clutches. "We can't be together."

"Why not?"

Seth studied me closely before saying, "It will never work."

"Why, Seth? Why won't it work?" I asked him angrily.

He grunted and stepped back from me. "Do you want to know why, Lily?"

I nodded and crossed my arms. "Yes! I

want to know!"

Without another word, Seth tilted his head back, and after releasing a soft cry, his wings started to emerge from his flesh. I watched in shock as they pushed their way out of his skin, ripping his shirt in the process. They kept growing until they were fully spread out. I gasped at the sight of them. Of course, I had seen them before — but never this close. The first time I saw his wings I thought they were intimidating, but now that I was getting a closer look at them, I realized they were actually quite amazing.

I took a careful step closer towards him. Seth eyed me warily, as if he were afraid I was going to freak out. I proved him wrong though when I placed a hand on his right wing, sliding my palm over the black feathers gently. They were silky soft, and I grinned when he flapped his wing, sending a gush of air in my face.

"Now do you understand why we can't be together, Lily?" Seth asked, faintly.

I shook my head at him and replied, "No. I don't understand. You have wings ... so what? It doesn't matter to me."

He glared at my response. "Stop being immature!"

"I'm not!" I shot back.

"How about when you age and I do not?" he asked. "People will notice, Lily. You can't live a normal life if you stay with me! I will only bring you unhappiness."

"I don't care ..." I whispered, meeting his eyes. "I love you, Seth."

With a deep sigh, Seth bowed his head and stared at the ground beneath his feet. "It doesn't matter if we love each other or not. The fact of the matter is, Lily, you're a human and I'm a demon. We aren't meant to be mixed."

"Says who?" I whispered painfully, a lone tear slipping down my cheek.

He glanced back at me, his eyes the blackest I'd ever seen them. "Says me."

"Seth, don't do this. Please!" I begged, reaching for him once more, but he avoided my hand and shook his head. "I need you ..."

"I'm sorry, Lilianna," he murmured. "I have to leave." Seth flapped his large wings and I cringed.

"No, please!" I cried out, my heart breaking. I felt absolutely helpless. If he flew away, there would be nothing I could do to stop him. "You can't go! You swore you would always protect me!"

I felt so pathetic at that moment. He was so calm about leaving me, yet I couldn't control myself. I couldn't help it. Seth was ripping out my heart and stomping on it. I was hopelessly in love with him.

"I will, Lily," he replied softly, the grey in his eyes returning once more. "I'll be watching you always... you just won't know it."

"But, Seth—" I began, my eyes crinkling from grief.

"Goodbye, Lilianna Mason," Seth whispered. "I will never forget you."

With one last heartbreaking look in my direction, he flapped his wings and flew high amongst the tree tops. He lingered in the sky for a few moments to stare down at me before he flew higher and disappeared, leaving me all alone on the forest floor. I didn't know what to do. I couldn't even move ... so I just stood there, staring dumbly at the bright blue sky.

A few minutes turned into thirty, and before I knew it the sun was setting. I was unsure why I was still standing in the same spot, gazing at the sky above. I guess I was holding out on the chance that Seth would change his mind and come back for me.

I ignored my parents' questions as I trudged up the stairs to my room. I just couldn't deal with them at the moment. They trailed behind me nonetheless, and it seemed my silence wasn't going to satisfy them. I had to lock my door to escape their badgering. If I told them the whole story, they wouldn't believe me anyway — and I didn't want to have to think up a plausible excuse for my absence right then. All I wanted to do the rest of the night was cry.

I exhaled deeply and stepped out onto my balcony, staring up at the night sky. Seth was really gone. That realization obliterated my heart. How was I going to get over him? I couldn't ... there was no way. Seth had showed me so many things — and loved me the way I'd always wanted to be loved. But there was nothing I could do about it. I would probably never see him again.

After taking a seat on one of the plastic patio chairs, I continued to watch the black sky. I wondered if Seth was up there now, flying around. Was he close by? But more importantly, was he thinking about me?

"Yes," a voice replied, breaking the silence and startling me completely. "He's always thinking about you, Lilianna …"

I twisted toward the arch above my balcony door, where a pair of glowing red eyes were staring down at me, cutting through the dark night. I jumped up from my chair and staggered backward in fear, hitting the railing of the balcony. My breath caught in my throat as the stranger carelessly jumped off the roof and landed in the open doorway.

The stranger was six-feet tall, with black hair that hung to the middle of his back, and ears that pointed at the ends. His eyes stopped glowing, but when I got a closer look at them, I realized they were actually almost an orange color, not red. He was wearing a tattered grey shroud and black jeans and shirt. There was something familiar about him, and that's when I realized he resembled Seth and Darcamius — though not nearly as attractive.

"Who are you?" I breathed anxiously.

The stranger smirked evilly, and it was then that I noticed two sharp fangs poking out of his mouth. He took a step in my direction, his head bowed so he could stare into my fear-stricken eyes.

"Who am I, Lilianna? I'm Krieel. Septhim's older brother," he hissed.

"Brother?" I replied warily. *More Darcamius' offspring? Great.*

He nodded with a toothy smile. "That's right."

In a flash, Krieel took a giant step towards me, invading the space between us. Before I had a chance to react, his hands shot out, grabbing me roughly by the shoulders. I screamed, shaking with terror as I stared up at him.

"What do you want?" I asked the demon fearfully.

His orange eyes flashed with delight as he replied darkly, "You."

About the author

Chelsea Lynn Charters was born in New Jersey, but was raised in Bay City, Michigan, before she moved to Florida at the age of ten. Chelsea is 21 years old and writes frequently, penning under her full name.

She has published one young adult novel, and has a short horror story published in an anthology.